¥¥¥¥¥¥¥¥¥¥¥¥¥¥¥¥¥¥¥¥¥¥¥¥

SILVER WINGS FOR VICKI

The CHERRY AMES Stories

Cherry Ames, Student Nurse
Cherry Ames, Senior Nurse
Cherry Ames, Army Nurse
Cherry Ames, Chief Nurse
Cherry Ames, Flight Nurse
Cherry Ames, Veterans' Nurse
Cherry Ames, Private Duty Nurse
Cherry Ames, Visiting Nurse
Cherry Ames, Cruise Nurse
Cherry Ames at Spencer
Cherry Ames, Night Supervisor
Cherry Ames, Mountaineer Nurse
Cherry Ames, Clinic Nurse
Cherry Ames, Dude Ranch Nurse
Cherry Ames, Rest Home Nurse
Cherry Ames, Country Doctor's Nurse
Cherry Ames, Boarding School Nurse

☆ ☆ ☆

The VICKI BARR Flight Stewardess Series

Silver Wings for Vicki
Vicki Finds the Answer
The Hidden Valley Mystery
The Secret of Magnolia Manor
The Clue of the Broken Blossom
Behind the White Veil
The Mystery at Hartwood House
Peril Over the Airport
The Mystery of the Vanishing Lady
The Search for the Missing Twin

Vicki inquiringly held up her manifest. . . . Surely this
was not the same man who had got off the plane!

Silver Wings for Vicki

SILVER WINGS FOR VICKI

BY HELEN WELLS

GROSSET & DUNLAP
PUBLISHERS
New York

I am grateful to
Miss Ruth Anderson,
Assistant Superintendent of Flight Stewardesses,
American Airlines, for the information
so generously given me in
the preparation of this book

CONTENTS

CHAPTER   PAGE

I   VICKI MAKES PLANS 1

II   BEGINNER'S LUCK 24

III   DISCOVERIES 36

IV   THE NEW CROWD 50

V   IN TRAINING 66

VI   GREAT DAY 83

VII   THREE IS A TEAM 100

VIII   THE MYSTERIOUS MR. BURTON . . . 117

IX   TROUBLES 129

X   THE NIGHT RUN 146

XI   GOING TO A PARTY 155

XII   THE FOURTH MAN 165

XIII   STREET OF SHADOWS 179

XIV   SMUGGLERS 193

XV   HOME IN TRIUMPH 201

SILVER WINGS FOR VICKI

CHAPTER I

Vicki Makes Plans

THERE IT WAS, BIG AS LIFE, IN THE FAIRVIEW SUNDAY paper. Vicki's hands shook a little as she spread out the newspaper on the grass under the apple tree, away from The Castle and Ginny's teasing. She read again:

To GIRLS WHO WOULD LIKE TO TRAVEL
To MEET PEOPLE—TO ADVENTURE

Vicki rolled over on her back and gazed up into space. Her eyes were as blue as the June sky overhead, this peaceful Sunday morning. Adventure! She sighed longingly. Yet no one could have appeared less adventurous than Vicki Barr. She was small, with a delicate, almost shy face, and soft ash-blonde hair. She seemed very fragile. But the fragility belied strong, wiry muscles and an amazing capacity for beefsteak. The dreaminess, if you looked closely, was more intentness, the absorbed look of a girl busy thinking up action—or mischief.

1

Her airy grace, the smallness and blondeness of her, made Vicki seem about as durable as a cream puff. Actually she was as sturdy as a young tree. She smoothed the skirt of her blue pinafore and sighed again. "If I apply for this flight job," she thought resentfully, "I know exactly what they'll tell me. 'Sorry, Miss Barr, but we think you look too young, too shy, and perhaps not strong enough.'"

With a glint in her soft blue eyes—not at all the sort of glint that goes with poetic eyes in a tangle of lashes —Vicki turned back to the advertisement.

"If you are twenty-one to twenty-eight, and single— if you are a registered nurse, or if you have at least two years of college or of business experience in dealing with people—then here's the most appealing job in the world! Apply tomorrow!"

Vicki had only two years of college, no business experience, and worst of all, she was under the age requirement. She nibbled sadly on a blade of grass. She wanted this job so much, so very much! Wasn't there any way around the requirements? Vicki put her mind to work.

Only two years of college. And her father, who was professor of economics at the near-by state university, was eager for her to complete the full four-year course. Persuading the professor to let her drop out of college would be a hurdle in itself.

Hm-m, no business experience. That was really difficult. But she had helped in the community-fund drive every autumn, sometimes garnering more pledges in her unbusinesslike way than even her father. She had helped run the day nursery on Saturday mornings—or didn't dealing with small fry count as dealing with people? Well, then, she had sold perfume at Frazier's last December when all the girls had taken jobs to make some Christmas money.

As for being too young, she could only pray for a lucky off-chance. Exceptions were sometimes made. "It doesn't hurt to hope. Or to try. They can only say no, and they *might* say yes!"

"*Must weigh,*" said the ad, "*from 100 to 125 pounds, and be between 5 feet and 5 feet 6 inches tall.*"

It made Vicki feel like something for the butcher's scale, but for once, being small was an asset.

"*Above all,*" the ad pursued, "*do you get along well with people? Do you sparkle?*"

Vicki pulled a strand of silvery-gold hair across her upper lip, making a mustache of it. She held it there and stroked it. The mustache was an infallible sign that Vicki was brooding. Sparkle? Well, did she? Vicki asked herself.

Freckles, the Barr family's spaniel, trotted up to her, ears swinging. He was a young gentleman, white with golden-brown spots, and flirtatious. He sniffed Vicki, sneezed, and backed off in indignation. Vicki stroked the silky ears but the dog reared back on his hind legs.

"You're wearing perfume again!" scoffed a young voice from The Castle's side steps. Vicki saw, from under the heavy-hanging apple boughs, her younger sister's short, browned legs running toward her. Vicki cautiously folded up the newspaper and sat on it.

"Freesia!" sniffed twelve-old Ginny. "Poor ol' Freckles. You know dogs hate perfume." She picked up the spaniel, who promptly licked her face.

Ginny was plump, sturdy, and—with her light hair in tight braids, braces on her teeth, corrective glasses, and orthopedic oxfords—distinctly unglamorous. Ginny looked exactly as Vicki had only a few short years back.

"Say, what are you doing here, lolling and daydreaming?" Ginny demanded.

"Secret." Vicki's voice was soft and gay.

"Tell me. I'll tell you a secret in exchange." Ginny put down the squirming spaniel.

"But it's really a secret, sweetie, understand?"

Ginny nodded her round little head and Vicki opened the newspaper to the full-page advertisement.

"Jeepers, it's tomorrow!" Ginny exclaimed. "Right here in Fairview! Every girl in town will be there, fighting to get in. Are you going to try for it?"

"Don't shriek so, baby! Ye-es, I'm—I'm going to try."

"Well, I hope they say yes," the twelve-year-old declared loyally; then added matter-of-factly, "But I bet they say no. You aren't the practical type, like me."

Vicki's small face turned pink. "Libel!" she retorted indignantly. "Who saved you when you trespassed on that meadow and the cow chased you? Who thought up an explanation about the time you spent all the money in your penny jar for lipstick?"

"You have your moments. But most of the time—" Ginny grinned blandly behind her spectacles. "Really, Vicki, you go floating around looking like a piece of bric-a-brac—dreaming with that idiotic mustache under your nose."

Vicki said with big-sister hauteur, "What was your secret?"

"Oh, that." Ginny examined her shoe. "Vicki, don't be mad when I tease you—you know I'd give anything to be just like you. It's just that you're so—so—" The little girl broke down.

Vicki pulled her gently down on the grass and put her arm around her. "You are a genuine, absolute sweetie-pie," she whispered into Ginny's ear.

Ginny hastily studied the newspaper, then stared perplexedly at her lovely sister. "How would you ever dare apply for something bold and brawny like this?"

"Listen," Vicki murmured. Far above them they heard the hum of a plane. Both girls looked up. A speck of silver streaked along in the blue.

Very softly Vicki said, "The sky . . . There is a

beautiful world up there. Clouds like frozen fountains, and endless blue, and the planets swinging in space."

"Vicki, have you gone crazy?"

"And the people! Exciting people, doing things that take them flying all over the world—presidents and scientists and soldiers and actors, men in gold turbans, engineers going far away to build, people living out the secret dramas of their lives—"

"I told you not to eat chocolate cake for breakfast! I knew it wouldn't agree with you!"

Vicki lay back on the grass, her slender bare arms under her bright head. "People have to dream, darling —dream, and make their dreams come true. Why, that's how the world goes on." Half to herself she added, "Dreams are expensive. But I'm willing to work hard for mine."

Ginny said flatly, "Here's my secret. I broke my new bike. Don't tell Dad."

"Very sad and I won't tell Dad. Ha! A poem."

But Ginny waited uneasily for something more. "I think it's the brake, Vic."

Vicki gave her a sidelong glance. "Of course, I'm the impractical type, you understand." She laughed and sat up. "It's out of sight in the garage, I presume? I'll take a look." She rose and walked across the lawn. It was an effortless walk, like a dancer's.

Ginny's gait was a bounce, and Ginny was humble. She watched in respectful silence as Vicki expertly slung the bicycle around, hunting for the trouble.

"You've jammed the brake, that's all," Vicki reassured her, "and bent these two teeth in the gear a bit. Hand me the pliers—no, the Number Two pliers." As she tugged on the brake, she grunted, "Just a useless, helpless dreamer. For this, you have to name all your children after me. Vicki One, Vicki Two, and Vicki Three."

"Suppose they're all boys?" Ginny retorted.

"Will you go chase yourself?" said Vicki. "No, by gum, I'll chase you myself!"

They zigzagged across the wide lawn, under the trees, around and around the birdbath, Ginny shrieking. The chase ended at the open kitchen door. Professor Barr's handsome, blond head popped out. Atop it towered a chef's cap.

"Would you rather have sauce Marguery or drawn lemon butter on the sole?" he asked, clutching a cookbook.

"No fish!" Ginny exclaimed.

"Which sauce is the more—m-m—epicurean?" Vicki asked.

"Ah, the Marguery!" her father answered. He grinned engagingly. "You take milk—or cream, if your mother doesn't catch me—flour, butter, sherry—seasoning, of course, but just a hint—" He smiled happily, his face pink with heat from the stove and satisfaction. "And your orders for dessert?"

"Chocolate cake," said Ginny. "Or what Vicki left of it."

"A pedestrian imagination." Professor Barr shook his head.

"*Profiterolles au chocolat*," suggested Vicki.

Her father's tall figure, tied securely in a chef's apron, moved out into the doorway. "I'm afraid that's beyond my powers. After all, I'm only a Sunday cook."

"Baked bananas with maraschino sauce, then?" Vicki offered demurely, and Ginny breathed insults.

The Sunday chef leafed through the cookbook. "Yes, here it is—" he cocked a knowing eyebrow at his elder daughter—"my little gourmet. But—ah—wouldn't you like a nice, simple bread pudding? I make a very successful bread pudding."

"I'd prefer Nesselrode pudding." Twin devils danced in Vicki's limpid eyes.

"Stop egging Dad on," called Mrs. Barr from the steps. Her cap of short curls enhanced her young face and active figure in the red sports dress. "Isn't it bad enough that he gets butter on the kitchen walls, honey on the gas cocks, and sugar crunching underfoot? How do you do it, Lewis?"

Ginny said, "It's a good thing you let him cook only on Sundays."

"We'd have no kitchen left, and no digestions, if we let Dad lose his amateur standing," Mrs. Barr remarked laughingly, as she rescued Freckles from a bee.

"Permit me to make three points," Professor Barr said, in his best lecture-room manner from the kitchen porch. "One, I am as good an amateur chef as any man in the Gourmet and Skillet Club. Two, this is my only hobby, recreation, or sin, as you prefer. Three, I will make Nesselrode pudding or bust in the attempt. Luncheon will be delayed indefinitely." He waved them away. "Ladies, go enjoy yourselves. Hey, Vic! Here's one recipe you don't know—*bombe glacé*, smarty."

And the chef returned to the kitchen, whistling. They heard him turn on a radio speech, then the egg beater whirred.

Ginny glared at Vicki. "You always get your way."

Their mother, overhearing, remarked, "Incidentally, Vicki, what is Nesselrode?"

"Oh, candied nuts and fruits and goo," Vicki replied absently.

"And where did you get acquainted with such fancy things?" Ginny demanded.

Vicki colored to the roots of her ash-blonde hair. "I read through Dad's cookbook one day when he wasn't home, so—" she grinned— "so I could be Dad's own little girl."

Ginny snorted. But Mrs. Barr nodded her curly head in approval and Freckles, always agreeable, wagged his stubby tail. Vicki was wondering whether she could count *l'affaire* Nesselrode as "dealing with people."

She longed to talk to her mother about that challenge

in the newspaper. It excited her so much that she felt like running and shouting. Betty Barr would understand: she still was a good horsewoman, and she sympathized with other people's enthusiasms.

But as for telling her mother— Vicki realized pensively that her chances of being accepted as a stewardess would be moderate at best. The competition in Fairview alone would be formidable—and the competition was nation-wide. No use alarming her parents too soon with her adventurous ideas.

So Vicki sat quietly on the sunny steps, but in imagination she was in a soaring plane with two men from the State Department. One of them glanced at the placard that read MISS V. BARR. He beckoned her up the aisle and said, above the four roaring motors: "When we land in Shannon, please help us to get on to London at once."

And the imaginary Vicki, in trim blue cap and suit, bent over him and said, "I've already made all arrangements for you, gentlemen."

The other hypothetical diplomat smiled up at her and waved a document bearing a heavy seal and ribbon.

"Your slip shows." Vicki jumped. This was not the imaginary statesman but Mrs. Barr reproving Ginny.

"Oh, Vicki," her mother said, "did you see this very interesting advertisement—the full-page one? I only wish I was within the age limit."

Vicki's heart thumped in response. Yes, her mother would understand—would approve! If— *If.*

"But what would Dad say? He'd never let you leave home," Ginny said wickedly, to her mother and aiming at Vicki.

Vicki did not dare stay any longer. She made the worst face she could at her small sister, and wandered off under the trees.

Vicki loved The Castle on its crest of hill at the edge of town. She had always felt it rare good luck to live in a place which all of Fairview drove out to admire. Not that the Barrs could afford a great deal on a professor's salary, even counting Mr. Barr's consultative services to businessmen's groups. But Cousin Bill had left the property to them, the biggest and best surprise the Barrs would ever have. When the Barrs moved in, it was rather a white elephant of a place, run down and gloomy. But, working with small means and plenty of enthusiasm, they had contrived to make the house a miniature castle indeed.

For The Castle—though not very large—had a tower, high Norman-casement windows, sloping red-tiled roof, an upstairs balcony, a buttressed oak entrance door. The grounds, too, resembled the park of a castle: a sweeping lawn setting the house well back off the road, spreading shade trees, a rock garden, a rose and peony garden, stone birdbaths and benches. Behind the house apple and cherry trees grew. Then the grassy hill rolled downward, became a little wood, and led steeply down to the lake. Professor Barr had built a boathouse down there, and a small dock.

Vicki glanced up at her own windows, with their prized balcony. The shadowy, pale-blue curtains in her room stirred a little.

"I would be stark, raving mad to leave The Castle," she thought in a rush of feeling.

Nevertheless, at nine o'clock Monday morning Vicki was in the lobby of Fairview's biggest hotel. Her silver-blonde hair was severely coiffed, to make her look older, she hoped. She had worn her gray suit, crisp white blouse and gloves, in an effort to tone down her Dresden-china prettiness and appear capable. Perhaps the very high heels were too frivolous, but they gave her a more dignified height—Vicki did not own a pair of sensible shoes, anyway.

"Where," she shakily asked the desk clerk, "are they interviewing for Federal Airlines?"

Directed to Suite 305, she went into an elevator. Five of her old classmates were already in the car, dressed with great care and eying one another.

"Hi, Vic," two or three of them greeted her in weak tones.

"Hi, yourselves," said Vicki. "Are you all praying like me?"

One big girl gulped, "This is the first time I ever applied for a job. I'm scared."

"You have lots of company," Vicki assured her.

The elevator door closed. They were all in too desperate and exalted a state of mind to be very sociable now.

The door to Suite 305 was wide open, and jammed with girls spilling out into the corridor. Vicki's enormous blue eyes opened wide and she was tempted to go right home. What a crowd! She recognized them from Fairview High School—this year's, last year's, year before last's graduating classes—Molly and Meg Murray from the village of Patoka, near by—a bevy of girls in baggy pastel sweaters and skirts from the state university—lively Jeanie Stone accompanied by two other girls, all with fresh, farm complexions—Jessie Naylor, very businesslike since acquiring her secretarial job—two pretty, efficient-looking redheads from the factory—

"They all look so determined and reliable!" Vicki thought, almost frightened, "Not—not *fluffy*, like me!"

She stood up as tall as she could and assumed a solemn expression, but that did not make her feel any braver. Pride alone kept her from fleeing out of the knot of girls in the corridor. Pride, and a young woman distributing numbers, one of which she handed to Vicki. With the numbered ticket in her hand, Vicki froze to the hotel carpet, trapped. She moved not on her own power but only as the line moved, slowly, silently forward. One by one the girls took seats inside the room.

Once seated, the secretary gave them application blanks to fill out. Vicki wrote hers on her wobbly knees, scowling over each question before she answered. Apparently Federal Airlines wanted to know everything except when she had had her first tooth. There were routine questions about name, address, relatives, citizenship, health, education, community activities. Then—and Vicki wrote in:

EXTRACURRICULAR—Dancing lead in school shows.

HOBBIES—Dancing. Candid camera.

LANGUAGES—Spanish, fluent. French, halting.

BUSINESS EXPERIENCE—None.

NURSING TRAINING—None.

FLYING EXPERIENCE—None.

Discouraged at three "nones," Vicki's pencil hesitated over the page. The next question sternly pressed her forward:

CHARACTER REFERENCES.

How dignified "Professor Lewis Marvell Barr" would look! Then she saw the phrase "other than relatives." After some rueful thinking, Vicki gave the names of her English teacher and the family doctor.

WHAT DO YOU READ? Considering the stacks of books and magazines that kept flowing into The Castle, Vicki could honestly list a good many titles, and a good variety.

ARE YOU WILLING TO WORK ANYWHERE IN THE WORLD? Vicki wrote joyously Yes!

The secretary collected applications as they were finished. Instantly Vicki was sure she had given the wrong, the most ill-considered answers. Well, all she could do now was to wait.

The all-morning waiting was agony. Meg Murray sailed into the inner room smiling and confident, and came out crestfallen. Her sister Molly went in and stayed such a long time that girls began to look knowingly at each other. Molly came out smiling much too brightly, and passed the line with her head held defiantly high. "No luck," the murmur went around. Three of the college girls went in and came out again so fast that some of the others, disheartened, dropped out, and Vicki moved up in the row of chairs. One of the farm girls emerged looking happy and expectant.

"How'd it go? Who's interviewing? Are they tough? Tell us!" they all whispered at her. The excited girl could only stammer, "Not tough, nice. I don't know anything for sure, yet. Good luck, kids!"

By now Vicki was second in line, hidden behind a tall girl. Vicki repowdered her nose, wet her lips, and tried to smile. The effect, she had no doubt, must be sickly. Then the protective wall of head and shoulders disappeared into the inner room, leaving Vicki exposed to that noncommittal, closed door. The low voices within told her nothing. She tried to recall all the intelligent, relevant arguments she had planned to offer as proof that the exact person Federal Airlines needed was Miss Victoria Barr. But her mind went even blanker than before. Out of the blankness the secretary said:

"Miss Barr, will you go in?"

Vicki walked into a confusing blaze of daylight. At a desk before the window sat a stunning young woman. Her hands were pressed over her eyes in a gesture of weariness. At Vicki's step she looked up instantly and smiled.

Vicki heard her own soft voice saying, "Shall I come back later—perhaps after you've had lunch?"

"No, thank you." Brilliant, searching, gray eyes smiled at her, and Vicki had an impression of sleek dark hair, artful make-up, a trim figure, style, and utter poise.

"My, what a frail-looking little blonde you are! But I'll bet you're really the wiry, hard-as-nails kind."

Vicki grinned. "And I can outeat any two boys."

"So that's why you spoke of lunch! But seriously, it was very thoughtful to suggest coming back later. That's exactly the sort of attitude I'm looking for in these dozens and dozens of girls."

Vicki was astonished—elated!

"Sit down, Miss—" the young woman glanced at Vicki's application form—"Miss Barr. I'm Ruth Benson, assistant superintendent of flight stewardesses for Federal Airlines. All the other supervisors interview, too." She leaned back more comfortably in her chair. "You see, we go out on interviewing trips before each new stewardess class starts. We set up in fifteen or twenty cities and hold interviews, as here. Sometimes we have publicity in the local paper, or sometimes girls write in to the airline asking for positions. We notify them of interviews, because the date's set in advance, and invite them."

Miss Benson said all this as if they were having a leisurely, friendly chat, not holding a business interview. However, Vicki realized she was under shrewd surveillance. She was careful to sit quiet in her chair, not fussing with hair or purse, hands relaxed in her lap.

"Sometimes"—Miss Benson chuckled a little—"I think that every girl in the United States wants to be a flight stewardess! Well, I did, myself." In reply to Vicki's quick look of interest, she said, "Yes, I flew for six years, and loved it. Why do you want to be an air stewardess, Miss Barr?"

Vicki leaned forward eagerly, lips parted—then remembered, just in time, that a business company was not interested in some girl's personal desire for flight and adventure, but in gaining a useful employee.

"Because I'd love to fly, and because I like people. I think I could be of service to air travelers and to the airline. Air transportation is growing so fast—I want to work into it and grow with it."

Miss Benson nodded her sleek head. "Refreshing to

hear a girl who *doesn't* say 'Because being a stewardess is such a glamorous job.' It's a demanding job. You must be able to handle all sorts of people, tactfully, in any sort of situation."

She asked Vicki questions about her friends, her life in Fairview, her family, probing for indications of tact and courtesy and poise. Vicki, her delicate face flushed, tried to answer briefly and modestly.

They talked about school subjects for a while. Miss Benson approved of Vicki's having had psychology, English, sociology, public speaking, because those things would help in the constant contact with people of all temperaments. Nursing training was usually an essential qualification, Miss Benson said "—because a flight stewardess often has to care for children and sick persons—" though an R.N. was not required by Federal at the moment. Had Vicki, perhaps, been a nurses' aide, or did she know first aid, or had she studied physiology or hygiene? Fortunately, Vicki had had training in both hygiene and first aid. Her nutrition and cooking courses would come in handy too, for serving meals aloft. Music, art, current events—all helped a girl keep up her end of conversation with all types of travelers. Miss Benson wished Vicki were better at languages, "because passengers are of all nationalities, and flight routes may take you into all countries. Good idea to brush up on geography, too, if your business is going to be travel."

"Very good," Ruth Benson said at last. "Very personable. You're a bit shy but that's pleasanter than being too aggressive. As long as you are resourceful enough— Now, stand up and walk around the room for me. I didn't really see you when you came in."

Vicki rose and circled the room, a small, graceful figure. In her imagination she was rather desperately humming a tune, and walking in time to it. That helped her keep her poise.

"Mm-hmm," said Miss Benson, and gestured Vicki to sit down again. "Yes, I think you could wear a uniform with some distinction." She scribbled something on a report sheet.

"May I ask a question?" Vicki ventured. "Everyone says stewardesses have to be beautiful. Is that true?"

The brilliant gray eyes glanced up. "Real beauty isn't necessary, but you have to be nice to look at: well groomed, pleasant, and not too tall or heavy. After all, a plane must carry the biggest payload possible, and the heavier the crew the less paying weight we can carry. Did you see that tall girl who came in ahead of you? She was qualified for this work in everything except that she's five feet eight and weighs proportionately. But the airlines do recognize that American girls are growing taller, and we're gradually raising the height and weight limits. Besides," continued Miss Benson cheerfully, "bigger, roomier planes are coming into use; and with bigger cabins there'll be space for taller girls."

She bent over Vicki's application and turned a page. "Oh, dear!"

Vicki's azure eyes flew wide open in alarm.

"You have only the minimum two years of college. And you have no business experience."

In the awful silence Vicki felt herself shrinking. "In a moment," she thought crazily, "I'll be as small as Alice in Wonderland when she drank the contents of that bottle." She opened her mouth to speak and no sound came out. But no one was going to help her but herself. It was now or never. She exerted a mighty effort and out came a quavering "Wouldn't you—ah— consider substitutes for a college degree and business?"

"What substitutes?" Ruth Benson encouraged.

Vicki described the home tutoring which Professor Barr had always given Ginny and herself, her various community jobs. Never until this moment had she realized how heavily all her experiences, so casually undertaken, were going to count someday. She pleaded her facts earnestly, as if Miss Benson were Gabriel holding the keys to heaven.

"We-ell," said Miss Benson, and swung around in her chair to look out the window into the street below. "That's pretty skimpy experience."

"But how is a beginner to get experience?" Vicki

gasped, seeing her hopes fade. "You can't get a job until you have experience, and you can't gain experience until you get a job!"

Miss Benson turned back with a wide grin. "All right, sell me on yourself. Go ahead. Let's see what you can do in a difficult situation."

Vicki clenched her small hands, lifted her head, and almost squeaked in her excitement:

"Even having a Ph.D., or being head of a business, wouldn't necessarily make a girl a good flight stewardess—unless she had the right personality!" A grin flickered across her face. "Getting along with people is like playing a game. You try to figure out each person and then—well—"

She told the interviewer about her approach to Professor Barr's sympathies via the cookbook.

"My head's swimming with sautés and baste and dice, and a lot of stuff I can't even pronounce, much less cook," Vicki confessed. "But that's my way of telling Dad I'm really interested in what he does—interested in *him*. And what do you know, he did fix me Nesselrode! Delicious, too." Vicki sighed reminiscently.

"Sold!" Miss Benson laughed. "Sympathetic interest in people is the first qualification of a good flight stewardess. Or," she added, with a smile, "of any charming woman."

Vicki sank back in her chair, gingerly congratulating herself. The gates of heaven creaked open a bit on their hinges.

"Yes, this is primarily a personality job," said Miss Benson. "But don't get your hopes up too high. Only thirty-five out of every thousand applicants are found acceptable for training, and then you have to pass your training exams, and a physical examination nearly as stringent as a pilot's. Besides . . ." She hesitated ominously, studying Vicki's application again, and fell silent.

Vicki's heart almost stopped beating. *Now* what was wrong?

"No, my dear. No. You're definitely not qualified. You're too young. We don't take anyone under twenty-one."

"But—but—but—I'm almost twenty-one, I'll be twenty-one in a few months. I'm mature for my age."

Miss Benson shook her head. "Not particularly. I *am* sorry."

Vicki was stunned. She slowly gathered up her purse and gloves. Miss Benson was staring at her. Vicki wanted only to get out of this room quickly. She was so terribly disappointed, she might burst into tears or blurt out something foolish before this knowing young woman.

"Very charming; pretty," Ruth Benson muttered. "Really interested in the business of air travel. Just a moment, Miss Barr."

"Yes," said Vicki numbly.

"I can't promise you anything. But once in a great while we make exceptions on one qualification or another." She glanced at Vicki's tense face and said sympathetically, "I'm sorry to keep you on tenterhooks. Ordinarily we tell an applicant no at once or engage her on the spot. But in your case, Miss Barr, I'll have to talk it over with our New York office. You'll have to wait until I get their verdict."

She rose and held out a strong, well-manicured hand. Vicki took it gratefully.

"Thank you, Miss Benson," she said from the bottom of her heart.

"I'll telephone New York so that you can have an answer as soon as possible."

Vicki left the hotel and started back to The Castle in a kind of daze, wondering how she could live through the hours or days while her future dangled in the balance.

CHAPTER II

Beginner's Luck

THE HANDSOME LATIN PUT HIS HAND ON THE SPEEDING plane's door. He would jump, he threatened, he would not go on living, if she persisted in being so heartless. "No, that's a shade too melodramatic," thought Vicki. She was sitting cross-legged under an oak on the wooded hill back of their house. She fitted her spine more comfortably against the tree trunk and started to revise her daydream.

The handsome Latin flagged her as she cautiously made her way down the aisle of the swaying plane. But Vicki did not like the handsome Latin very much, after all. Very well— A bell rang faintly, continuously. Another passenger was summoning her. With a polite nod to the disappointed young man, she moved farther down the aisle. There sat a paunchy middle-aged man, his lap full of photographs. He studied the girl with piercing eyes. "Turn your profile," he ordered. "Have you had any acting experience?"

Vicki sighed. "Possible if not probable. It's actually happened to stewardesses. Doggone that bell—our phone, I guess. Oh, my stars, maybe it's for me—maybe it's Miss Benson—"

She was on her feet in one leap, running fleetly up the wooded hill, flashing in and out between the trees, hair streaming. "Here I am!" she shouted. "Don't let them hang up!"

Her mother appeared for a moment on the side steps. "It was only Mr. Brown asking if we'd want butter and eggs from his farm this week end," she said, and disappeared.

Vicki bit her lip. Freckles galloped up, but Vicki felt so discouraged that she would not even look at him. The spaniel's feelings were hurt. His liquid eyes reproached her, his bit of tail wagged only tentatively.

"Oh, all right," Vicki said, and threw a twig for him. "No use making you feel bad, too."

Freckles bounded down the driveway and out of sight beyond a hedge. He returned presently, walking sociably beside the mailman.

Vicki let out a moan and ran once more. "Mr. Wiggins! Oh-h, Mr. Wiggins! What have you got for me?"

"Expectin' a love letter?"

"No, more important!"

"Well, here's a letter for your mother, a free sample of smelling salts for Ginny, a magazine advertisement for your dad—"

"Don't *do* this to me," Vicki begged.

"Now don't you hurry me, young lady. A free sample of dog biscuit for Ginny *and* a letter for you."

Vicki tore it open immediately. It was a notification that Frazier's Department Store would consider restoring her to the perfume counter.

"It's fate, warning me," Vicki thought wretchedly. "Oh, pooh, it's no such thing. I won't be superstitious." She wadded the letter into a ball and let Freckles chew up her only career possibility to date.

The Barrs' telephone rang again, the long, insistent shrilling of a long-distance call. This time Vicki got there first. It was Miss Benson, calling from another city.

"Miss Barr? I have good news for you. The verdict is yes!"

Vicki let out a whoop of delight that brought her mother hurrying into the hallway. Ginny peeked in from the kitchen.

"Of course, Miss Barr, you will have to prove during the training period that you are mature enough. And you must bring with you a letter of permission signed by both your parents."

"Yes, Miss Benson! Of course! Certainly!" Vicki promised wildly, wondering what her parents were going to say. Her mother stood by, looking puzzled.

"The airline will give you a free flight to New York," Miss Benson's crisp voice went on. "You'll leave this

Saturday from Chicago on the six P.M. plane. I'll mail your tickets and instructions, air mail, right away. Is that all clear, now?"

"Yes, Miss Benson, it's clear—and it's wonderful! Oh, thank you, thank you!"

"I'll see you in New York," Miss Benson said. "Have a good flight."

Professor Barr opened the door of his study and appeared at the top of the stairs, holding a book.

"What's all the whooping and hollering about?" he asked.

"Who's phoning you long-distance?" Mrs. Barr inquired.

"It's—a friend, a supervisor—that is—"

At this point Ginny emerged with a peanut-butter sandwich and a wise expression. The twelve-year-old planted herself where she could see and hear everything. Vicki gulped.

"Well, as a matter of fact, Mother and Dad, I have something to tell you," she started. "To ask you—I mean, if you—"

"Don't tell me you've still got that Chriscraft on your mind?" her mother groaned.

"Naw," said Ginny, her mouth full.

"You're going away," her father said cautiously.

"If I have your okay—to New York—my very first flight—this Saturday—" Vicki sputtered. Then she threw out her arms and cried, "It's wonderful! I'm going to be an airline stewardess! If you'll give your permission. Come into the living room, all of you, and let me tell you about it!"

"Well, I'll be hornswoggled," said Professor Barr, half an hour later. He was impressed by the idea but still couldn't get used to it. And he had about run out of arguments. "I'd like you to complete your schooling," he went on, "but we're all individuals. If this is your great opportunity—I'm disappointed, Victoria, but I wouldn't stand in your way."

Mrs. Barr was even pinker than Vicki. Freckles had caught the excitement, too, and his tail thumped the carpet. The only unruffled Barr was Ginny, very dignified on the couch.

"Looks like Vicki's going," she commented.

"All right," Professor Barr said reluctantly. "Mother and I will write the letter of permission. You didn't want to go on with college anyway and I suppose, while this is risky, you could fall out of a tree right here at home."

"It's not a bit dangerous," Mrs. Barr corrected, shaking her curls. "There's a lower percentage of flight accidents than auto accidents. Not even as dangerous as me on that half-broken mare I've been training for the Curtises."

Vicki hugged her mother and cried, "Let me get a word in edgewise! Jehosaphat, isn't it marvelous! Did you ever hear of such luck!"

"Beginner's luck," said Ginny. "You haven't ever been up, even. You'll prob'ly be airsick."

Vicki ran over and yanked her pigtails. There would have been a tussle, except that Ginny threw her arms around her sister, shouting, "Hurray for you! Hurray!" The tussle turned into a furious waltz around the living room.

"This calls for a celebration!" Professor Barr exclaimed, enthusiastic at last. "Wait—I'll make grape-juice punch and my special whatcha-ma-call-ums. We'll all toast Vicki!"

"Make plenty of punch!" laughed Mrs. Barr, starting for the hallway, "because I'm going to call up all our friends!"

Friends began to trickle into The Castle—family friends, Vicki's schoolmates, neighbors. Word spread. Even a reporter from the Fairview *News* bustled in, wrote up Fairview's first flight stewardess, and snapped a picture of Vicki.

When that picture appeared next morning—a very satisfactory one, Vicki considered, since it made her look five years older and nothing like herself—the telephone started to ring. It rang and rang, all day and all evening, and so did the doorbell. Vicki was torn between pride, embarrassment, excitement, and plain fatigue. Freckles, who had assumed the job of greeting all visitors, was one exhausted little dog. Even imperturbable Ginny found it advisable to escape, at intervals, into the branches of the apple tree to rest.

Vicki's hopes of getting some packing done and her thoughts sorted out were swept aside in the excitement. And Saturday was only day after tomorrow! She announced she would duck whenever the bell rang, and locked herself in the room she shared with Ginny. She took inventory of her closet and bureau, made lists of what to take along, lists of people to whom she must write thank-you notes for their going-away gifts, and read again the letter that had followed Miss Benson's telephone call:

"Here are your plane tickets. You are allowed forty pounds of luggage. You will need clothes for classes at the Stewardess School, a coat to wear on the airfield, clothes for your free time in New York. Publicity pictures probably will be taken. Please do *not* have a permanent wave."

Vicki did not understand that last stipulation, but obediently dug out and packed what clothes she had. She longed to buy a new dress, but it was not really necessary since—joy—she would soon be in that pert blue uniform.

"Besides," she thought, as she stuffed stockings into slippers, "I'll soon be able to buy a new dress *out of my own salary!* Imagine not having to ask Dad for things. Being master of my fate and captain of my own pocketbook." She foresaw bankbooks with her name on them, an apartment with her name beside the bell, herself nonchalantly signing a check. "I s'pose I'll have to make out an income tax report, too," she thought importantly, and giggled.

By Friday evening she was ready. Callers had been discouraged, for this was Vicki's last evening with her family, her last few hours at home.

She could not eat much. After supper she wandered about the house. She would miss the long, hospitable living room, with its fireplace and shining brass andirons at the far end; the long, ancient, gray-velvet couch that eight of her crowd could squeeze onto; the bowls of garden flowers her mother set around; the rows of high casement windows that let in such a curious, dusky, sun-dappled light. She turned, sighing. In the dining room, the faces of her family were sharply outlined against the French windows, which stood open to the twilight. That sharp picture imprinted itself on Vicki's heart. She went into the hall and started up the stairs.

Vicki liked the spiral staircase, inside the tower, and the tower window almost best of all. She paused halfway up to gaze through the many-paned window into the trees with their nests of wrens, sparrows, and thrushes. Every spring she and Ginny spread out crumbs and grain for the bird families on their return north. They were twittering sleepily now, as the last rays of the sun dipped over the hill.

The upstairs rooms were quiet, still warm and

fragrant from the heat of the June day. Vicki paused at the open door of her mother and father's bedroom. When *she* got married and was mistress of a household, *she* was going to have a four-poster bed and framed samplers like her mother's. At the corner bedroom, with its closed door, Vicki hesitated. Here Cousin Bill, builder of The Castle and the Barrs' good angel, had lain for three years, and here he had died. Remembering a spunky, very brown-eyed old man, Vicki did not open this door. Instead, she went into her and Ginny's room, and sat down before her desk to think.

What would it be like—this new life? She was stepping into the unknown. Perhaps, as her father had said, she might not even like it. Or she might be airsick—horrible thought. But that was only Ginny's expert teasing. Or she might simply fail to do the job well enough. The whole adventure, cloudlike, might blow away into nothing.

"I won't fail," Vicki promised herself with youthful confidence. She thought of the new world of the sky, its airy domains opening to more and more people—of all it meant to be earthbound no longer—of the lives, busy or troubled or gay or lonely, which hers would touch on the earth-circling silver ships.

Vicki shivered. "I can't fail. I mustn't. And I know I won't! I feel *good* about this, deep down inside. I knew all the studying and growing up must be leading to something—and this is it. This is *right*."

Her parents seemed to think so, too, on that last quiet evening together. If they had misgivings, where Vicki had only blind confidence and rapture, they were too wise to say so. Even Ginny forbore to tease. It was a strangely moving evening for Vicki.

Going to bed in the blue room for the last time caught at her feelings, too. Ginny was already half asleep in one of the twin beds. A single lamp burned. Vicki moved softly.

"I'm not asleep," Ginny mumbled. "You may be a pest at times, but I sure am going to miss you. Staying in this room with your bed empty—"

"Ah, baby." Vicki had not realized that going away would hurt so much. "Have Freckles sleep on my bed. I mean it. I'll try to persuade Mother."

"Mm-m. A lot of good Freckles is. Can't talk to *him*."

Ginny was crying. But when Vicki discovered it, the little girl fiercely denied being such a sissy.

The next day, Saturday, was a whirlwind: last-minute chores; good-bye to the garden and the birds; the clock spinning irrationally. Suddenly it was time for good-bye to her mother and Ginny and Freckles.

"Take good care of yourself, dear," her mother begged. "Keep away from the propellers and don't eat hamburgers."

"I will, darling—I mean, I won't." Vicki clutched hat, gloves, purse, overnight bag, a box of candy, and her mother.

"Send me a picture of you in your uniform!" Ginny gulped.

"And all the free samples I can lay hands on!" They exchanged large kisses.

Freckles had crawled under the couch in a sad mood and had to be fished out for his farewell.

"Good-bye! Good-bye!" Vicki cried to them from the car, and she and her father spun down the driveway. Out on the road they swung north into the state highway, driving fast. To Vicki, it felt as though they were already soaring. If the car had taken off into the golden air, she would not have been surprised. Anything was possible on this day of beginnings!

It was a long, fast drive to Chicago. Professor Barr did not talk much, but kept his eyes on the unwinding ribbon of road and the cars and trucks whizzing past them. Vicki was beyond talking. Each familiar town they went through, each well-remembered farm or field receding behind them, pushed her closer and closer to a silver plane. Her hair whipped in the wind and her heart beat wildly.

They reached the airport at a quarter to six. A great field with clusters of planes everywhere, crowds of people, a glass-enclosed signal tower—Vicki did not know where to look first! Her father chuckled and took her firmly by the elbow. He piloted her through the busy air station, verified her reservation with a brisk, blue-uniformed girl not much older than Vicki, had her luggage weighed and ticketed, told Vicki's weight to the passenger agent. Then they went to stand with other travelers before a roped-off door.

"There's your plane," Professor Barr whispered.

By standing on tiptoe Vicki could see, only twenty yards from her, a huge, glistening ship spreading its wings. It looked a bit clumsy on the ground, its nose tilted up, its cabin windows at the wrong slant, its tail squatting on the earth. It was built to soar, not to sit down, Vicki reflected. But even then, as young men hustled lovingly around the ship, filling up the gasoline tanks, loading suitcases and mailsacks aboard, the plane was beautiful.

"Your name, please?"

An attractive young woman in stewardess's uniform and cap moved smilingly among the passengers, checking off a list of names.

"Barr? Yes. Your name, madam?"

Vicki looked tremulously at her father. He put his arm around her shoulders encouragingly.

The rope was pulled aside. The stewardess waved them toward the plane.

"Aboard, please!"

CHAPTER III

Discoveries

THE PASSENGERS SURGED ONTO THE WINDY AIRFIELD.
With the others, Vicki waited a moment in the shadow
of the great plane. One by one, they started up the
steps. Vicki climbed up too, hesitating at the plane
door where the hostess crossed off each passenger's
name.

Vicki ducked her head to go through the low, steel
door and climbed up the aisle of the steeply slanting
cabin. Here were rows of deep, reclining leather
chairs, two together on the left side of the aisle, single
seats on the right. Vicki pulled herself along by grasp-
ing seat backs, and found a single seat midway in the
ship. She tossed her hat and overnight bag into the luggage rack overhead, and sank excitedly into the
luxurious leather chair. But she couldn't see out the
little oblong window. She pushed the curtains aside,
perched on the very edge of her chair, and peered out.
A broad, long, silver wing stretched outside her win-

dow. Vicki's heart turned over with joy at the sight of it. Then she saw her father, hanging over the wire fence, beaming and waving. Vicki waved back. Other passengers brushed past her. Up in the front of the plane was a small glass sign, lighted from behind:

NO SMOKING
FASTEN YOUR SEAT BELT

Vicki fumbled around the sides of the chair but couldn't find any straps. What a novice she was! As the stewardess came up the aisle, Vicki embarrassedly touched her blue sleeve.

"Where's the belt, please?"

Cool hands and a smiling face bent over her. "Here you are." Vicki was sitting on it.

Vicki took the two wide straps, which were fastened to the arms of the chair, and buckled them firmly across her waist. As she leaned to wave again to her father, deep-throated roars startled her. The motors had awakened, the propellers ahead spun and flashed. The whole plane started to vibrate, as if it were alive. Vicki's blood surged with excitement—throbbed and pulsed with this mighty plane.

Now the engines sang louder, more insistently. The passengers, strapped in, settled back in their seats. At the back of the cabin, the steel door slammed shut. The hostess moved up and down the aisle, offering a box of chewing gum.

"Take a piece," she advised Vicki. "It'll keep you swallowing and that relieves the pressure on your eardrums."

Vicki chewed, and listened to the ever-mounting hum of the engines. The plane stood still, gathering power. It roared, it trembled, yet did not lift. Like a straining giant, it vibrated with accumulated, unbearable power, until Vicki, holding her breath, thought it would explode.

Then the plane rolled smoothly down the runway. Vicki looked out and was astonished to see her father's figure diminishing beneath her. They had risen so gently that she had felt nothing at all! The airfield streaked past. Hangar roofs slid away under them. They climbed, and evening clouds appeared out of the sky to meet them.

Vicki sat speechless, released, overwhelmed. So this was flying. This was what people talked about with shining eyes and never were quite able to express. This wonder. This miracle. This beauty and power and awe-struck joy at being set free in the air.

Clouds like blue veils drifted by. The plane skimmed along at fantastic speed, rocking gently from side to side. Vicki turned to see if the other passengers were as thrilled as herself. The lighted sign, she saw, had gone off, and several people were smoking and reading the evening newspaper. A man up ahead was dozing. Behind, a woman was writing a letter.

But the girl directly across the aisle sat with face aglow. Vicki glanced at her sympathetically. She was about Vicki's own age or a bit older, athletic looking, with crisp brown hair cut almost like a boy's, and bright brown eyes in a lively face. She had, Vicki noticed, an air of self-reliance: she obviously knew how to take care of herself. Yet she was very feminine and attractive.

Then the plane rose higher, bouncing like a rubber ball. Vicki suddenly was conscious of her stomach. She caught sight of a cloth pocket sewed onto the chair back before her, and its contents. One item was a large, heavy brown-paper bag.

"I *won't* be sick," she groaned. "I just won't ruin my career at the very start. O-o-oh, I feel bad."

The girl across the aisle touched Vicki's elbow.

"Open your air vent." She pointed up.

Above her window, Vicki located a metal disk with a tiny knob. She slid the ventilator open halfway and cold, gusty air blew in on her. Immediately she felt better.

"Thanks." She smiled.

"There's been a rainstorm in Minnesota and this wind is the tail end of it," the lively looking girl called above the engine noise. "We're almost through it now, and then, I think, the going will be smooth as glass. This is unusual."

"Do you fly a lot?"

"Some." It was difficult to talk across the aisle over the roaring engines, and the conversation lapsed. Vicki, chewing earnestly on her gum, wondered about this girl who flew. She looked ready to burst with suppressed excitement.

Outside, the sun was dropping. Long shadows crept over the countryside below, but it was still bright daylight up here. They were flying smoothly now. Vicki poked into the chair pocket and found flight time-tables, travel literature, thin air-mail writing paper with the Federal Airlines emblem on it.

"Wouldn't you like some dinner?" asked a pleasant voice. There stood the stewardess, proffering a tray. She took a small white pillow from the luggage rack, laid it on Vicki's knees, and set the tray firmly on that. Vicki settled down happily to inspect the plastic dishes and tiny salt and pepper shakers, with the same flight emblem on them. The silver, however, was sterling, and the tray and dinner napkins were of fine linen. It took a little managing to eat soup when the plane swayed, but Vicki discovered the trick was to fill the spoon only half full. The dinner itself was steak with all the fixings, piping hot and delicious. Even that meticulous chef, Professor Barr, would have approved. Vicki had just finished her coffee and ice cream, and was opening the waxed-paper envelope with its mints and cigarette, when the stewardess appeared and took Vicki's tray.

"Did you enjoy your dinner?"

"Very much! How long do we fly before getting in to New York?" Vicki hoped there would be hours and hours more of this entrancing experience.

"We fly all evening. We're right on schedule, too. You'll be in New York early enough to get a full night's sleep!" The stewardess smiled. "You're Miss Cox, aren't you? And you're going to be a flight stewardess, I understand?"

Vicki, puzzled, said yes to the second question, "but I'm Vicki Barr. Who is—?"

"I'm Jean Cox," the girl across the aisle sang out.

"And I had named *you* Barr." The stewardess laughed. "I'll come back to you girls later, and we'll talk." She moved away.

Vicki and the other girl grinned at each other.

"So you're going to be—" "You, too?" they said in unison, and laughed.

"When did you know—" "Don't you adore flying?" they shouted across the aisle, and laughed again.

The fat man beside Jean Cox rose gingerly from his chair. "Would you like to trade seats?" he offered.

"Oh, thank you!" Vicki exclaimed.

"Thank you, sir," Jean Cox echoed.

There was a scramble as they changed places. Vicki sank down beside Jean Cox.

"Well! Hello! Congratulations!" They shook hands like two long-lost friends.

Jean shook her cropped brown head. "This is luck!
I was wishing for someone to talk to about this stewardess miracle. I'm so excited that if I don't talk, I'll
burst!"

Vicki's blue eyes twinkled. "*You're* excited! Why,
I'm practically in pieces. This is my very first flight!
You've already flown, at least."

"Haven't flown much in luxury like this." Jean
waved a tanned hand at the carpeted, upholstered
cabin of the soaring air liner.

"What have you flown in?" Vicki visualized army
transports, dirigibles—what else? Her imagination
faltered at kites, which comprised all her past experience with flying.

Jean screwed up her face. "Oh—I—just fly. A little."

"*You mean you fly your own plane?*" Vicki gasped.

Jean examined her shoe, in the same embarrassed,
offhand way that Ginny would have. "Uh-huh."

"You *own* a plane?" Vicki was breathless.

"A little Piper Cub. It's painted yellow. It goes only
fifty or sixty miles an hour." Jean grinned. "If there's
a sixty-mile wind, it flies backwards."

Even inexperienced Vicki had to giggle at this.
"But—how come you fly?"

Jean slid down in her seat. "Thought it would be
fun. So I went out to the airport and took lessons."

Vicki absorbed this, round-eyed. "When," she inquired in awe, "did you start learning?"

"When I was about eight." Jean cocked a mischievous eye at Vicki. "My parents didn't mind. Matter of fact, they learned right along with me. The crazy, flying Coxes, they call us. We have two little planes in the family. That's about all we have got. One's my sister's. Hers is a stunt plane."

By now Vicki was prepared for any shock. She gulped and asked, "How old is your sister?"

"Twelve."

"That's Ginny's age." They proceeded to a rueful and appreciative comparison of notes on younger sisters. Vicki interrupted to ask Jean if she had ever been airsick.

"Yes." said Jean frankly, "but I outgrew it." The conversation went on to their families, friends, school, and what Stewardess School might be like. Jean casually admitted to having done some barnstorming.

"You'd be good at that—stunts, I mean," she said suddenly to Vicki. "You're little and wiry and quick, and I'll bet that behind that dreamy expression there's plenty of nerve."

"Thanks," said Vicki, with a smile like a sunburst "Thanks a lot. Uh—I like you, too."

"Okay, pal," Jean smiled. "It's a deal."

And thus everything was settled. From then on, they were Cox and Barr, friends, partners, a team.

The stewardess, coming forward in the plane, found the silver-blonde head and the cropped brown one close together.

"Hello, there." She perched on the aisle arm of

Vicki's chair. "Everyone," she glanced around watchfully, "seems to be comfortable. Now I can take a little time with you."

She smiled and Vicki thought her one of the pleasantest people she had ever seen. The stewardess had intelligence in her pretty face, dignity in her bearing. She radiated friendliness. It occurred to Vicki that Miss Marcella Kramer—that was the name on the placard—probably was a typical stewardess.

Vicki asked her, "Do you think anyone as green as I am will ever manage to be a flight stewardess?"

"Of course you will," said Jean stoutly, and Miss Kramer said:

"Don't worry, the airline will train you."

"This work is fun, isn't it?" Jean asked eagerly.

"It's hard, isn't it?" Vicki demanded.

Miss Kramer dimpled. "Well, being a flight stewardess means hours on your feet, catching sleep at odd times, staying over in strange towns, eating irregularly, being away from home. And besides feeding and caring for your passengers, you have to keep your plane in good order during the trip. But"—she touched the silver wings pinned to her jacket—"I wouldn't change jobs with anyone! Honestly, it's the most fun I ever had. The passengers are such a varied, colorful lot. Every flight is different. You never know from day to day what's coming next!"

"Any romance?" Jean teased.

The stewardess laughed. "Too much of it, sometimes. Can't get your work done. And you do meet
simply everybody, traveling like this."

"Are air passengers special in any way?" Vicki
wanted to know.

"Oh, yes! They're an exciting and glamorous lot, as
a rule—people who do things. Movie stars, celebrities,
executives—people at crises in their lives—why, I've
even had an FBI man hot on the trail of a mystery!"

"Mystery!" Vicki breathed. Her lashes brushed her
cheek as she thought, "Yes, anything could happen on
a plane."

Jean murmured, "And the stewardess is in sole
charge."

"*That's* who is really in charge," said Miss Kramer,
nodding toward the front of the cabin.

Through the door from the cockpit came a
responsible-looking man of thirty, in pilot's navy-blue
uniform and cap. He looked around at the passengers
with an almost fatherly air.

"Everything all right?" he asked the stewardess.

"Everything's fine, boss," Miss Kramer replied. "Did
I bring you enough dinner?"

"Yes, but I could use more coffee."

Pilot and stewardess walked to the back of the cabin,
looking very much a team, Vicki thought. They disappeared into the tiny kitchen.

Vicki whispered to Jean, "Who's flying the ship while the pilot drinks coffee?"

"Copilot, silly. And the pilot isn't drinking coffee because he likes refreshments. He works hard up there, and the monotonous propeller noise and the dim night light make him sleepy. So he needs coffee as a stimulant. The stewardess has to look out for her two boys up front."

"What about the poor lone copilot right now?"

"Didn't you notice the stewardess unlocking the cockpit door and bringing them coffee a couple of times? Maybe the copilot will come back here, too, and stretch his legs."

They were nearly at their destination, Jean said, when the pilot returned forward, and then another young man appeared. The copilot, or first officer, immediately impressed Vicki. He was quite young, only about twenty-three, tall, lean, rather wind-blown, and with a look on his face which arrested her. It was a grave look, and his clear eyes seemed to focus on great distances. He was an airman, a new breed to Vicki. He strode past them, unseeing.

"Handsome," Jean muttered. "A born flier, you can see it."

"I'd like to know someone who looks like that," Vicki confessed.

"We'll probably meet all the pilots, in time," Jean said easily. "That is, *if* we pass the training course. Goodness, do you know we're nearly there?"

Vicki sighed. She wanted this floating idyll to last indefinitely. The plane was getting to New York much too soon to suit her.

Now below them appeared, at more and more frequent intervals, the widespread lights of big towns. Presently an enormous area of lights blazed out of the darkness. It looked like millions of jewels twinkling for miles and miles. The other passengers were putting away their books and newspapers, crushing out cigarettes. The lighted sign went on again. Everyone strapped in.

Vicki strapped too, with a sigh. "Here's hoping my first flight won't be my last. I want *more*."

Something odd happened to her stomach. It seemed to be creeping up into her throat. The plane was coming down to a lower altitude, and reducing its speed. Vicki remembered to swallow. She looked out the window and was startled to see tops of skyscrapers whip past. Then they were over a river full of lighted ships and in a scant minute zoomed over the airport.

Flying in a huge circle, they gradually dropped lower and lower. Now objects on the ground enlarged to their normal size, and Vicki could see men running on the field, automobiles, parked planes, the glinting glass of the control tower. They floated low over the length of the field, then almost imperceptibly their wheels touched ground. They were down!

After that, all was happy confusion to Vicki. She and Jean walked down portable steps, Miss Kramer tucked them into a crew car, and they rolled along a busy suburban highway toward Manhattan Island. Back across the river, and they were in the heart of New York. Here were tall buildings, beautiful streets, myriad lights, crowds of people, excitement in the air. Vicki gasped.

"Where are we going? Miss Benson wrote me about a hotel but I never expected— Jean, look!"

The driver chuckled. "Impressed, aren't you? Well, you have reason to be. Federal Airlines is mighty proud of its hostesses, so they are put up at one of the best hotels. Wish somebody'd pay *my* hotel bills for me."

The crew car pulled up before a great building on a wide avenue. Within were beautiful lobbies, well-dressed people, strains of dance music. Vicki was so dazzled that Jean took charge laughingly and did all the arranging for them both.

"Here, register," she said, joggling Vicki's elbow.

Vicki tore her gaze away from a white-haired woman in a white evening gown and signed the hotel register.

"Glamour, I never met you till now," she said, when the door was flung open to the room she and Jean were to share. "Look at that view!" She went over to the open window and hung out. "Oh-h—New York!"

"Careful, we're on the fortieth floor," Jean warned. "Say, there's nothing wrong with this room, either. Will you kindly look at this dressing table?"

"And the twin lounge chairs!"

"Whee! The Queen of Sheba had nothing on us!" Jean threw herself flat on one of the beds, moaning, "Oh, bliss. Oh, bliss."

Vicki sobered. She remarked in a small, meek voice, "You know, we're going to have to *earn* all this. This isn't Christmas, Cox."

"Yep." Jean sobered too and got off the bed. "Guess it behooves us to go right to bed, and right to sleep, so we can get right up tomorrow and see some of the sights of New York before we buckle down to work."

"Right," answered Vicki, and they went off into giggles of joy and excitement.

Ten minutes later their lights were out and the two would-be flight stewardesses were snuggled into the twin beds. Jean fell asleep instantly, her face in the pillow. But Vicki stared drowsily into the dimness, too happy to want to sleep, savoring the last of this wonderful day.

The silver plane—the clouds—the night sky—the girl in blue—what a voyage it had been. And now this tall, brilliant city—why, the very reflections in the window shimmered like—shimmered like—diamonds and like silver planes—like silver—like—

Vicki slept.

CHAPTER IV

The New Crowd

EARLY MONDAY MORNING VICKI AND JEAN RELUCTANTLY abandoned beds, breakfast, and the beautiful hotel to report to Stewardess School.

"Now we begin!" Vicki exulted. "Now! The real thing! The only trouble is"—she stopped to yawn—"it feels so early in the morning this morning."

"Never mind that. First we conquer subways to get to Stewardess School."

Jean, brisk and wide awake, and a sleepy Vicki trotted out into the New York streets, and dived into the subway. They battled through swirling crowds of people, through a confusion of roaring trains, asked their way through a series of escalators and platforms.

"My freshly pressed suit!" Vicki moaned. "Your stepped-on shoes! When they see us at the school, they won't let us in."

"Be nonchalant like me," Jean replied blithely. "I'm

50

an old hand at subways. Been in New York often with my father."

"If you're always as cheerful as this, at practically the crack of dawn," Vicki observed bitterly, "we can bid each other farewell right now, Miss Cox. Or is it a family curse?"

"You'll be cheerful at six A.M., when you're an air stewardess—oh, yes, you will!"

"When I'm a—! Did you know would-be's like us are dropped if we don't make good in training?"

"Did you know it's a really stiff course?"

The train sped out of the tunnel, presently, and up into daylight. Now they were riding through pleasant suburbs. The end of the line was Flushing, where the Stewardess School of Federal Airlines was located.

The two aspirants wandered along the quiet tree-shaded streets until they came to the right address—a large, brown office building.

"Where are the planes?" Vicki asked, disappointed. "All I see is a grocery and a drugstore."

"This isn't the airport, my landlubber. This is the school. Come on."

"Coming. Let's pray. Pray hard."

They climbed stairs and discovered that two entire floors were tenanted by Federal Airlines. Here were classrooms, offices, rooms full of drafting tables with blueprints of planes tacked on the walls, an experimental kitchen.

A huge propeller lay in the hall. Then they found several men in shirt sleeves, clusters of girls, some knowing, some obviously new like Vicki, and a few poised young women in stewardess uniforms. Everyone greeted everyone else; the atmosphere was like that of a club. Vicki and Jean walked through awkwardly, feeling very much out of it and wishing very much to be included.

"Are you new here?" said a voice behind them. "Can I help you?"

The two girls turned and saw a vivacious young woman in uniform smiling at them. Her voice and manner were so gracious that Vicki's heart promptly melted.

"You're going to be part of the new class, aren't you?" the young woman went on. "I'm Nan Connor, your instructor. So glad to know you! If you'll just report to the chief instructor's office at the end of the hall, and then to Classroom Four—"

They thanked her and hurried off, feeling heartened.

"May I tag along with you?" someone else said bashfully. "I need moral support."

A sweet-faced young woman approached Vicki and Jean. Vicki smiled at her, and said:

"We haven't an ounce of moral support between us, but you can be scared along with us if you like. It's cozier that way."

"Pooh, who's scared?" said Jean, and immediately answered herself: "I am."

The three girls introduced themselves. The new-comer's name was Charmion Wilson. She was taller than the other two, of fair coloring, and Vicki sensed a certain sadness in her.

In the chief instructor's office they found, milling around a desk, another dozen girls as untried and eager as themselves. Vicki peeked over shoulders and saw a calm young woman in blue uniform, writing.

"Sign this list, please," she said, "and then take the blanks to fill out." She, too, had such a gracious friendliness that the words sounded sympathetic, encouraging, and welcoming all at once.

Charmion Wilson said softly to Vicki, "Why does she wear the uniform for a desk job? Do you suppose she's flown?"

The young chief instructor looked up and smiled. "I couldn't help hearing. Yes, all the instructors have been stewardesses. I've flown a hundred thousand miles."

A dramatic-looking brunette gave a little shriek. "How could you ever, ever have given it up? To fly—to live in the clouds—and then to drop back to earth! So unromantic!"

The chief instructor grinned. "On the contrary, quite romantic. I got married. That grounded me."

The brunette gasped. "Air stewardesses can't marry? What is the airline thinking of?"

"Of business," snapped a reddish-haired girl.

There was an abrupt silence. The young woman at

the desk covered the awkward moment by saying, "Take blanks, girls, and fill them out, please . . . Classroom Four. And good luck to you candidates!"

They all moved along the corridors searching for Classroom 4. Jean demanded under her breath: "Who's that Madam Trouble?" Charmion Wilson read aloud from the blank: "For Publicity Information. What musical instruments do you play? Have you ever done any flying? Complexion? Personality? Home-town newspaper? Do you talk in your sleep? Do you prefer light meat or dark?" She laughed nervously. "No, no, those last two questions aren't really in there!"

Vicki giggled, but as she walked along she was absorbed in studying the girls around her. So these attractive girls in sports clothes were to be her classmates, her competitors, and perhaps someday her comrades in flight! They seemed a pleasant, well-mannered lot, not very different from Vicki herself, except for their varying accents—southern, western, eastern. Vicki suddenly noticed one other difference. They were all older. Some wore college sorority pins.

"Oh, oh," Vicki groaned to herself, "I'm going to be the baby of the class. I must be the only one in the class who needed a letter of permission from Mama and Papa!"

At the door of a large classroom, Vicki headed for the back row of chairs—as far out of sight as she could get. Jean and Charmion followed her, unaware of the frantic thoughts going on in that ash-blonde head.

Girls continued to troop into the training room. Vicki looked at them, and at the diagrams of planes on wall and blackboard, and then at a girl who sat down beside her.

"Good mornin'," the girl said. "It's a right pretty mornin' for a new start, isn't it?" Her voice was slurred and southern, her face pretty as a china doll's. "I'm Celia Trimble and I do hope you don't mind me speakin' to you. I'm so lonesome and excited and all, it's like Christmas almost, but on the other hand, it isn't." She smiled brilliantly at Vicki and seemed to expect an answer.

Vicki gulped and wondered what the right answer was. "I feel the same way as you do" seemed to be satisfactory. And Vicki did sympathize with anyone who was in the same boots as herself.

The lively instructor, Nan Connor, hustled in, flashing a smile at all of them. She mounted the platform, tossed back her wavy hair, clasped her hands behind her back, and announced:

"Anyone who thinks being a stewardess is an easy, romantic job, go away! Go away right now!"

No one stirred. Someone giggled, immediately stopped. Nan Connor looked at them all with piercing eyes.

"This isn't glamorous—this is hard work. Don't think you'll have Sundays and holidays off. This is the transportation business." Suddenly she grinned at the listening girls. "But for fun and excitement, I wouldn't trade flying for anything in the world! All right, now you know the worst and the best. Let's get to work."

In rapid succession she pointed to the parts of the plane on the diagram and named each one. "Pilot's compartment. Cargo compartment. Cabin. Passengers' entrance. Engine. Reversible-pitch propeller. Landing flap. Main landing wheels and retracted nose wheel."

Then Nan Connor unrolled a marked wall map. "These are the routes. Memorize 'em. New York to Nashville to Houston. Chicago to New York to Boston. St. Louis to Des Moines to San Francisco. Newfoundland to New York to Washington. New York to Mexico City. That's only a few."

Vicki's eyes shone. All the girls were staring, trying to keep pace with the information being thrown at them. There was a commotion out in the hall. Someone out there dropped something heavy on the floor.

"Now or never, by golly!" a man's voice exploded. "Galloping Caesar, I haven't got all day!"

Jean whispered to Vicki, "Sounds like he's going to cloud up and rain on somebody."

The commotion grew louder. Nan Connor gave up trying to ignore it. She went to the door and said, "All right, all right, Clarence. Come in. They're all yours."

Clarence turned out to be tall, skinny, lugubrious, and a photographer. With him was an attractive young man, in whose battered hat was stuck a card which read PRESS.

"Ladies," Clarence croaked, "Federal Airlines wants your pitchers in the papers, and a nice li'l story about how good you can cook, or how you're a duke's daughter incog—incog—in disguise, see, or somepin'. This here is Pete Carmody, he's a newspaperman, but he can't help it, so be nice to him and tell 'im the stuff. All right, now, fix your faces and line up against the back wall."

The girls looked at one another in amazement. "Are we working girls or are we movie stars?" Charmion asked. She was clearly too reticent to enjoy all this fuss. Pretty Celia declared it was "a nuisance but thrilling," and could Vicki lend her a mirror? Clarence herded the candidates against the wall, while Nan Connor fumed and the young newspaperman cocked his head at them speculatively. Vicki felt silly but she squeezed out a smile, and held it.

"You might as well get used to this," Nan Connor called out. "Stewardesses have to do lots of publicity work. You represent Federal to the public. You'll symbolize the girl in aviation. So look pretty, please. And prepare yourselves to lecture at high schools on flying, and give interviews, and—"

"Ready!" Clarence bawled to the thirty-five waiting girls. "Here, you—" he pointed a bony finger at Vicki —"stand up here in front. And you—" he dragged

Charmion forth—"whatcha mean hidin' like that?"

He turned to the reddish-haired girl and the dramatic brunette who had clashed in the office. "What you two fightin' about? For the center place? This ain't the movies, you ain't prima donnas, you know! Now in the name of home and mother an' Federal Airlines, *stand still* and SMILE!"

The photographer took several pictures, getting crosser and crosser. The girls smiled like angels and made faces at Clarence between shots.

Nan Connor said, "Take the little blonde, she's the youngest in the class. There's a story for you, Pete."

Vicki flushed to her ears. Jean said, "Aha! Baby of the class, huh? Just wait—" Fortunately at that moment the dark girl cried: "Take me too! I'm an actress!"

"Actress? Where've yuh acted?" Clarence said cynically, while the newsman grinned.

"In summer stock. I have, too! And a blonde and brunette together will make a good picture!"

Clarence shrugged and waved her over beside Vicki.

"I'm Tessa, what's your name?" the dark girl whispered.

Vicki had to smile at all that eagerness. "Vicki. How shall we pose?"

"Look, I'll show you." Tessa put her arm around Vicki, flung back her head, pretended to laugh, and said out of the corner of her mouth, "That's one of the poses I learned in dramatic school. You put your arm around me, too, and laugh like anything. Or look intense!"

Vicki's laughter was genuine. Tessa was a character!

Nan Connor called, "Take a picture of Mrs. Wilson. Her husband was the famous test pilot."

Charmion Wilson stepped forward. Vicki and Jean exchanged a glance. So Charmion was a widow! And she was hardly older than Vicki herself. Charmion smiled obediently for the photographer, then went to look out the window by herself. Her back was very straight.

"Is Peggy Crile here today?" Nan Connor asked. "I'm sorry I don't know all of you by name yet. Clarence, what about taking—"

Vicki thought Charmion looked very much alone. She went over to the window, and put her arm through the other girl's.

Charmion smiled bravely at her. "I want to fly, like him. The airline waived the no-marriage rule for me."

"Good for you," said Jean Cox, who had come up to stand sturdily beside them. "You must be very proud."

Charmion, not looking at them, said, "It's only a month since Hank was killed. In a ground accident, as you probably read. We weren't married very long."

There was a silence.

"Charmion," Vicki said, "I have an idea—if it appeals to you. You're staying at the same hotel where all the class is staying, aren't you?" Charmion nodded. "Have you a roommate?" Charmion said no and began to look eager.

"Well," Vicki pursued, "Jean Cox and I share a room, and next door there's a single room vacant. It would be fun to have you next door. Will you move in—if we can get permission?" She pressed Charmion's arm warmly. "Please do."

"I— Yes, thank you. I'd like to."

Jean said earnestly, "Miss Connor didn't mean to— remind you. She probably was trying to pay you a compliment."

Charmion smiled. "People are so careful not to mention Hank—as if I were thinking of anything else."

The alert young newspaperman had discovered something was going on. He came up to the three girls and addressed Charmion.

"Mrs. Wilson? I don't want to intrude, but any time you feel like talking about— Well, he was a great flier and my paper would like to honor him."

"Thank you," Charmion said. "Some other time. Just let me get started here—"

Vicki and Jean glared at him. "Go away," Jean said. "Let her alone."

"Now, that's not nice of you," Pete Carmody said, unruffled. "I'm sure Goldilocks here wouldn't talk like that."

"I would and I will," Vicki hissed at him. *"Go away."*

"Lovely," said Pete Carmody. "Just lovely. Such eyes and hair. Speak French? Love children? Want to go on the stage?"

"I don't want to go on the stage," Vicki retorted, "and I don't want to be interviewed either."

"Spunkier than she looks," Pete Carmody mumbled, scribbling it down on his writing pad. "Name? You'd better tell me, Federal will spank . . . Ah, thank you. You'll see me again, Miss Barr."

Vicki gave him her No. 3 Frozen Smile.

"Yes, you *will* see me again," he said, eyes sparkling, and strolled away, hat jammed on the back of his head.

Vicki was astonished, and a little curious. She had never met anyone quite so cocky before, nor seen such a beat-up hat, at least, not on anyone's head. And yet Pete Carmody was likable. Maybe newspaper people had to be bold to do their job. He was the second young man of a new breed whom she had recently encountered. The first was the nameless copilot on the flight to New York.

With Clarence and Pete Carmody finally out of the way, the class settled down again. Nan Connor resumed her lecture. It was like a college class, but with a professional air.

"A stewardess with passengers in her plane," Miss Connor explained. "is like a hostess entertaining guests in her own home. She sees that they are comfortable, chats with them, serves them meals. More than that, the stewardess looks out for her passengers, really takes care of them.

"Once my flight was canceled and three of my passengers wandered away to a movie," Nan Connor related. "Half an hour later, the flight was reinstated and I had to scamper about to round up my charges. You can't just mislay twenty-one, or forty-nine, or sixty passengers."

The class laughed outright.

"Another thing. You must make trips through the plane at fifteen-minute intervals. A passenger might think you were busy and not want to call you. So you come around to him. You're there *for* the passengers!"

Everyone looked solemn and responsible.

"Don't ever, *ever* fall asleep on the job! You mustn't have too many dates and too little sleep. Remember that flying at high altitudes means less oxygen in the air to breathe, and that makes you sleepy. One girl fell asleep at fourteen thousand feet—the pilot had to fly that high to avoid rough air—and while she was asleep one of her passengers lost consciousness from lack of oxygen. If she had been awake, she could have given him oxygen. That man nearly died."

Now the girls looked sober. Celia, beside Vicki, seemed positively scared. Nan Connor hastened to add:

"Anoxemia happens very seldom. When you see a passenger breathing hard, just give him oxygen. Watch for first riders. They're fun to have aboard. One night it was so cold and drafty that the carpet was going up and down on the plane floor. I saw a great big fat man simply freezing. He didn't know we always have blankets and pillows on the overhead racks, and hot coffee in the galley. And he didn't want to 'bother' me. Well, you can be sure I saw to it that he was comfortable, just to show him!"

The reddish-haired girl raised her hand. "Maybe he didn't want to admit he was a first rider."

"That's right. You girls will have to be tactful. You might say 'Mr. Smith'—always call your passengers by name—'have you flown this route before? Do you fly with Federal very often?' You can go on to say 'You might like to know, Mr. Smith, that there's a ventilator here, for fresh air, here's your buzzer to call me, and there are snacks aboard if you get hungry.' "

"Sounds nice," Jean Cox spoke up. "Super-de luxe!"

"Well, that's the whole idea—the stewardess should make the trip so pleasant that the passengers will want to fly with Federal again. You are Federal's diplomat."

Nan Connor paused for breath, and asked if there were any questions so far.

The aggressive reddish-haired girl again raised her hand.

"What is the passing grade in this course?"

The young instructor looked surprised. The girls had been listening raptly, flying and conversing with passengers with her—all, apparently, except this canny, businesslike girl.

"Ninety-five per cent is passing. Ninety-four fails." The class murmured.

"Ninety-seven is the highest you can get. There's no such thing as one hundred per cent. You'll have a weekly quiz. Yes, Miss—Miss—?"

"Dot Crowley," said the same aggressive candidate. "I don't see why someone couldn't get one hundred per cent. Someone who's flown and traveled a lot, and has a high I.Q., and plenty of executive ability and self-confidence—"

Miss Connor was looking at her curiously. Her classmates, too, shook their heads. Dot Crowley had a steely set to her jaw that warned people away. Nan Connor said carefully:

"That's a good question, Miss Crowley. You mentioned executive ability and self-confidence. Those are fine traits, in the right place. But what you need for this job is tact. Above everything else, you must be able to get along well with people! For example, if a girl can't get along with her own classmates, we wonder how she'll get along with the passengers."

Vicki recognized this as a warning to Dot Crowley. Miss Connor must have noticed the incident in the office, and later the one with Tessa in front of the photographer!

Dot Crowley shrugged, looking neither to left nor to right. "I don't see what that has to do with it."

Miss Connor drew a deep breath and walked to the other end of the platform. "Any further questions?"

Tessa's hand fluttered up.

"Isn't it time for lunch?"

That broke the tension. The whole room laughed. Nan Connor agreed with Tessa, and the class adjourned. The first "get-acquainted" session, the most difficult, was over.

CHAPTER V

In Training

THE DRUGSTORE WAS "THE PLACE." BY THE TIME VICKI got downstairs and into the drugstore, she had collected quite a little crowd at her heels: Jean, of course; Charmion, who needed sympathy and understanding; Celia tagging along and prattling; and Tessa. They settled themselves at a table for six, and started chattering all at the same time.

Jean shook her cropped head at Vicki. "The baby of the class. And here I've been treating you like an equal, you—you infant! Impostor!"

Charmion teased, "Eat a big lunch, Vicki, and maybe you'll grow."

Tessa and Celia were already debating whether a sarsaparilla malted would taste good or would send them to the infirmary.

At the counter, all by herself, sat Dot Crowley. Vicki felt sorry for her, and at the same time exasperated with such stiff-necked behavior. Besides, she was curious to learn whether the chip on Dotty's shoulder would come off. She stared at Dot and Dot turned around.

Their eyes met. Dot glared; Vicki managed to keep on looking pleasant. Then Dot's eyes fell on the vacant chair at their table for six. Vicki smiled an invitation. She did not mean to, particularly; she simply could not help being friendly any more than Freckles could help wagging his tail at all comers.

"What are you doing?" Tessa said in a horrified whisper. "We don't want *her*."

Celia said unexpectedly, "It's not nice to have cliques."

"An act of faith?" There was understanding in Charmion's sad eyes. "Vicki, I think you attract people to you."

Dot Crowley had come up to their table.

"Let me attract you to this vacant chair, Dot," Vicki suggested. "Do we all know names? Jean, Tessa—"

Jean was polite to Dot, but resigned, not friendly. Vicki gave her a verbal prod. "Jean, my love, how's about sharing your menu with our Big Executive here?"

Jean's mouth twitched with laughter. She handed over the menu.

"It's all right. Go ahead and laugh," Dot said. "I deserve it. I never can remember that I have too much push and a trigger temper. I never put the brakes on in time." She sighed and wriggled in her chair.

"Maybe we'll reform you," Vicki said lightly.

The six girls who began lunch as strangers ended it as friends—at least, by taking an interest in one another. They could not help being fascinated by accents alone—Vicki came from Illinois, Jean from Minnesota, Celia from Florida. Dot hailed from Texas, Charmion came originally from New Hampshire, and Tessa had grown up right here in New York. Quite a large part of the United States was represented in their little group.

There were more classes after lunch. The indefatigable Nan Connor lectured them on air-mail routes, cruising ranges and speeds, gasoline capacity, types of motors, landing speed and distance, oxygen system, wing spread. Passengers always asked questions about these, and the stewardess had to know the answers. Passengers often turned out to be learned persons, or even airplane engineers, so the girls would have to study hard.

"Don't worry," Miss Connor said. "Once you start to fly, you'll get to know these things without half trying. A little later in the course, we'll go out to see the airport, and have lessons from the pilots. That's fun!"

In addition, Miss Connor asked them casually, would they please read, every week, from cover to cover, eight specified national magazines, "so you can discuss the news intelligently with your passengers, and carry on a civilized conversation." But, she warned them, discussing did not mean arguing, and they would be wise to avoid controversial subjects.

Then Nan Connor gave the girls an extraordinary caution.

"You're going to meet all sorts of people traveling on your plane. Most of them are grand but—watch out! We've caught criminals hoping to make a fast getaway—we've apprehended people smuggling stolen goods, or illegal goods, like narcotics—or carrying dangerous cargo, like dynamite, which could send your ship up in fireworks. Be on the alert at all times for suspicious characters!"

Vicki was sitting straight up in her chair, electrified. This was something she had not expected.

"I am not joking," Miss Connor reiterated soberly. "I am telling you the plain facts. Warning you. Anything, *anything at all,* might happen on your plane."

Then the young instructor went on matter-of-factly to other training topics. It took Vicki several minutes to calm down and get her imagination under control after that startling warning. But Miss Connor expected them to take this, or anything, in their stride. They were to be literally women of the world, Vicki remembered.

By late afternoon, that first day, Vicki had heard so

many new facts that she was dizzy. But she felt, too, that she had grown up considerably in even one day of this round-the-world atmosphere.

The next thing was to get Charmion moved in next door to herself and Jean.

Jean was all for the move and when Vicki told Miss Connor the reason, the instructor immediately gave permission, and telephoned the hotel. The single room adjoining Vicki and Jean's was reserved for Charmion.

On the ride back to Manhattan in the subway, the newly formed trio rejoiced. "Cox, Barr, and Wilson," Jean said. "We sound like a law firm." She curled her fists before her eyes to form imaginary spectacles, and said in a gruff voice, "Will the junior partner kindly wake up?" and prodded Vicki with her elbow.

"The junior partner is awfully tired, and besides, will the middle partner— Whoops, we sound like the Three Bears."

The two of them giggled and joked, trying to cheer Charmion. The young widow smiled a little and said above the subway noise, "You're nice to put up with an old lady like me." It turned out that she was six months older than Jean, who was six months older than Vicki. They reminded Vicki that no matter how old she grew she would always be Junior to them, and that they would always be happy to advise her from the height of their superior age and wisdom.

Vicki thanked them profusely.

With Charmion installed next door, they became a trio in earnest. They went through the usual feminine routine of trying on one another's clothes and rearranging hair-dos. They compared notes on tastes and ambitions, hotly debating everything from boys to movies to planes, and back again. There was only one subject they never mentioned: Charmion's brief and tragic marriage. She did not want to talk about it, and the other two did not press her.

"But I wish she would talk," Jean said to Vicki late one night as they lay in the twin beds in the dark. "It would relieve her to get it off her chest."

Vicki said slowly, "Maybe Charmion will tell us eventually, when she's ready. Anyway, I think she looks brighter these last few days—and that's the important thing."

"She's a darling," Jean mumbled in her pillow.

"We seem to be good for her," Vicki said. "We take her mind off the past." She thought about Charmion in relation to the other girls. "Maybe if *she* could help some one—Dot, for example—it might make her feel better. What do you think?"

Jean's only answer was steady breathing.

That was the beginning of what Jean later referred to as the Barr Nothing Intrigue. It was by design, Vicki hoped, that Charmion could be lifted out of the solitude of her grief. There was no design, however, in the way the other girls of the class came drifting from their various floors in the hotel to congregate in Vicki's room. For, no matter how personalities might strike sparks, somehow Vicki's room provided neutral ground.

"It's too darn peaceful," Tessa burst out on Sunday afternoon, when it was raining and their trip to the Statue of Liberty had to be abandoned. "I'd enjoy even a fight!"

"You can try me. It would take an angel to like me," boasted Dot.

"See my wings?" Vicki waved her arms. "Anyhow, you're not as fiery and fascinating as you pretend. That's Tessa's department—she's trained for it. Speaking of wings, when do we go up?"

"I can hardly wait," pretty Celia Trimble said. "I'm pinin' away to go up."

"You mean 'go upstairs,'" Jean corrected. "You want to be professional when you meet those handsome pilots, don't you?"

Celia and the others giggled at this but Charmion said nothing. She kept her eyes on her hands, twisting the wedding ring on her finger. The tall, slender girl, though seated on the bed among the others, seemed entirely alone.

Dot Crowley said, "I think you're all being silly. The pilots probably are old married men, and bored to death with stewardesses."

"The copilots, then. They're younger," Celia said hopefully.

"Airmen! Men of action and daring!" Tessa shook back her dark hair. "After my world of make-believe, to find men whose *real* lives are sheer drama— Please don't laugh at me. I mean it."

"You're a bunch of romantic idiots," Dot sniffed again.

Vicki saw her chance, "Charmion, what do you think about that?"

Charmion roused, and smiled. "I think Dot probably will be Cupid's first casualty."

"Why?" The reddish head bobbed in indignation. "You tell me why!"

"Because, Dot, you resist so." Charmion hesitated. "You're so ferocious about *not* wanting friendships and romance that I wonder— Come over here and I'll tell you what I mean." She spoke with a new animation. Dot rose and went over, perhaps out of nothing more than vanity or curiosity, but she did sit down amicably at Charmion's side.

Vicki felt warmly satisfied, until she saw Jean's brown face with a wicked, knowing grin on it.

"I caught you," Jean whispered.

"Will you go take a nice, long, refreshing drink of shellac!"

"Why, thank you, and do join me. Seriously, Vic," Jean whispered, "it will be interesting to see if you can kill two birds with each other."

Vicki relayed some of this nonsense in her letters home, describing her new friends and work. In return came letters, boxes of cookies, clean laundry, and several highly satisfactory visits with her family via long-distance telephone.

Classes continued. There were fascinating lessons in how to heat and serve precooked meals aloft, how to handle any small fry or animals on the plane, and should the plane have to make an overnight, unscheduled landing, how to put the passengers on trains or into a hotel and keep them comfortable and happy. Although such things as aerodynamics, flying on a radio beam, and mail versus passenger weights were discussed, the great topic was people—people and travel. Most of the girls loved both, and loved flying. That was why they labored so hard and eagerly on the weekly quizzes, and evening after evening recited aloud to one another in their hotel rooms, and drew maps even with their eyes closed.

By the end of the third week, halfway through the course, the girls were getting restless. Vicki felt that if she did not get another taste soon of that marvelous sensation called flying she would take off all by herself on nothing more than will power. It was a relief when Nan Connor announced finally that they were going to the airport. She also promised them a grand surprise later in the course, but smilingly refused to tell what it was.

The great New York airport dazzled Vicki. When she and Jean Cox had arrived that first night they had been whisked away to the hotel immediately. Now,

ın broad daylight, the class was going through the airport, from the great driveway where all roads con-
verged to the inner offices, with Nan Connor explaining everything as they went along.

First came the vast semicircle of handsome buildings, embracing the big asphalt field, and beyond, the
marine base for seaplanes on European runs. The class
walked along the ramp, or boardwalk, in the sun and
wind; from here, visitors could see planes arriving,
taking off, being parked, being tuned up and loaded.
Every single minute, a silver speck roared in, a great
ship vanished in the blue.

"This is the busiest place I ever saw in all my born
days!" Celia Trimble shouted above the zooming of
the planes.

"Look at the stewardess—the one boarding that
four-engine job!"

"Look at the men in turbans getting on her plane!"

"There goes one of Federal's flagships—away
down at the far end of the runway! Watch it—it's going to taxi past us— Here it comes— Whee! There
go its wheels off the ground! It's lifting! It's up—
it's up!"

The girls bent back their heads till their necks
nearly cracked, to see the great ship soar and thunder
right over them. It was so near they could see the
pilot's face, and the steel rivets in the wings. In a split
second, it was but an echo and a pale dot in the sun-
shiny sky.

Nan Connor grinned at Vicki. "Thrilled?"

"This is the most beautiful, wonderful, exciting thing I ever saw! If I don't pass the course *now*—!"

"We're going to start our tour, girls," Nan Connor called out. She pointed to the glass control tower, with the beacon lights for night, atop the Administration Building facing the center of the field. "We're going up there! Come along!"

They entered the Administration Building. Its huge lobby, with murals depicting earth and the heavens, was the terminal for many airlines. Here were passengers, passenger agents and freight agents, girls in uniform behind reservations desks, switchboards, telegraph desks, and restaurants. There were shops of every sort here, banks, offices of airline, oil, wheat, railroad, finance, and other companies. Miss Connor told them that ten thousand employees, some private, some governmental, worked here.

They went on to the traffic control tower. This glass-enclosed tower was the nerve center of the airport. Here were complicated instrument panels and dials and radios; here were men holding lists of schedules and aeronautical charts, and talking into hand microphones. These dispatchers directed the take-offs and landings of the swarming planes outside. No pilot could take off or land without their permission.

"Outgoing, Trip Eleven. This is New York Control Tower. St. Louis Sixty-seven. Two thousand. Cleared to intertraffic pattern. Traffic west. Runway Twenty-one. Report crossing Dervish Point. Over."

Out of the loud-speaker suddenly came a man's voice: "De Long calling New York."

"New York," said the control man into his microphone.

"De Long in Flight Ten, coming in over Manhattan at five thousand. Estimate arrive in three minutes."

The control man repeated the pilot's message back to him. "All clear." Then another signal buzzed him and he spoke again. "Incoming, Trip Thirty-two. No runway for you yet. Keep circling at three thousand."

A second later the St. Louis plane lifted and passed the glass tower. Minute after minute, these traffic men of the air cleared planes in and out, one at a time, on widely spaced airways, thus avoiding collisions. At night, in fog, in rain, snow, or ice, the girls were told, their work was of critical importance. In weather when a pilot could not see his hand before his face, the control tower directed planes down to safe landings by radio, within an inch of the right parking spot. The pilot relied on instruments and radio.

They went on to the radio room, and here Vicki watched shirt-sleeved men wearing earphones and operating another sort of instrument panels. Corresponding instrument panels were in the cockpits of the planes. These radiomen were sending the pilots, in Morse code by radio beam, directions for navigation,

weather reports, traffic information. Eastbound planes
fly at odd thousands of feet of elevation, Vicki learned,
while westbound traffic flies at even altitudes. Civil
air regulations, fixed by the government's Civil Aeronautics Authority, made standard rules for all to
follow.

While Vicki listened to this avalanche of technical
information she noticed with amusement how the different girls were absorbing it. Jean Cox's eyes shone;
Charmion and Dot, standing together, listened closely,
learning; but poor Celia and Tessa and several others
were obviously having a hard time. All this was as
new and strange to them as it was to Vicki. However,
Vicki saw nothing particularly difficult about these
plain-as-day principles. And she never had been fooled
by the old prejudice that if you happened to be a girl
you did not quite have good sense. Vicki watched, listened, understood—and enjoyed it.

"Bet I could work one of those contraptions," she
thought. Her fingers itched for machinery.

The class trooped to the weather-forecasting rooms,
where meteorologists marked blank maps with whorls
and codes, predicting wind, weather, and visibility for
the pilots. Nan Connor said passengers invariably
asked the stewardess a million questions about
weather. Then the girls walked downstairs to the
maintenance hangars, where sat rows of enormous
plane motors getting the routine nine-day overhaul.

Clambering over planes were dozens of overalled mechanics and technicians. Vicki found out that if and when she went to work in the sky, there would be a ground crew of from five to ten persons to keep her plane in condition. She saw men with microscopes testing machinery parts for flaws. She saw a scientific laboratory where new planes, gasolines, radios were being invented.

By lunchtime Tessa was frankly holding her head. "De-icers, antennae, airlanes, cloud formations—! And I thought we came out to the airport to meet the pilots!"

After lunch, eaten on a terrace restaurant while planes flew over their tables, they did meet the chief pilot. He was a pleasant, graying man who reassured the girls that all the things they learned today would eventually form an orderly, simple pattern in their minds. He gave them a brief lecture on the principles of flight, explaining how the forward speed and the air-cutting shape of the wings and tail kept the plane up. "Not very different from flying a kite," Vicki whispered to Jean.

The chief pilot particularly warned the girls about the danger of the propellers, which revolved so fast that they became invisible. "You are not used to being around planes," he cautioned them. "Be careful when you walk across the field toward a plane that is warming up. Never walk under the wings of a plane when the motors are running. Never run after a hat blowing along the ground or you'll be led into the propeller."

A tall, wind-blown, young man came in to speak to the chief pilot. It was the same young flier who had impressed Vicki on her flight to New York.

The chief pilot was busy answering questions so the young man waited at the door, beside Vicki. She wished he would speak to her. After all, they were practically coworkers. He did speak.

"Didn't I see you on my plane about three weeks ago?"

"You have a good memory," Vicki smiled.

"I noticed you because you seemed to be enjoying the flight so much." His eyes were grave, examining her. They were a flier's eyes, impersonal, steady, pre-occupied.

"It was my first flight. I loved it."

His lean face broke into a smile. "Hope you pass the course, then."

Vicki looked respectfully at this young man. She wished he might say he would be glad to have her aboard his plane. But he said nothing further. The best she could think of to say was, "You haven't told me your name."

"Dean Fletcher. Copilot."

"I'm Vicki Barr. Hopeful candidate."

"Hello." They grinned at each other.

Then the chief pilot began to gather up his papers.

Dean Fletcher said "Excuse me" to Vicki and hurried forward.

"Huh!" said Dot. "What are you thinking about?"

"I was just thinking," Vicki said, "some boys are so far from being ladies' men that if you hinted delicately for flowers they'd probably bring you a potted plant."

"Hm-m," said Jean, and grinned.

For the next hour, the thirty-five girls went through a parked plane, in small groups. Each group took its turn inspecting the galley, or sky kitchen, and also practiced making up berths. Vicki waited in the sun and wind on the busy field with her group.

At last it was their turn. They were the last group to climb the portable steps to the passenger cabin. The enormous plane thrilled Vicki. While she explored various compartments she dreamed of playing hostess to dozens of people on this beautifully appointed ship.

Then the chief pilot called all the girls together at a safe distance from the plane and at one side of it. He directed ground men to rev—revolve—the four propellers, then signaled one of the pilots to start the engines, one after another, until all four were roaring. He wanted the girls to see the power, the danger, the wind and dust being whipped up, to impress it upon them, so that they would protect themselves and their passengers at landings and take-offs. Over the din of engines, the chief pilot shouted explanations.

That impressively ended the lesson for the day.

Now the girls were free to go home, but no one wanted to leave the airport. They wandered through the thronged buildings, then outdoors along the visitors' deck, and watched the planes arrive and depart. Vicki's group of six hung over the deck rail, fascinated by "the beauty treatment," Tessa said, which mechanics gave a waiting plane.

"Imagine," they said to one another, "we'll be flying! We'll be part of all this!"

"Imagine!" Vicki echoed. And she thought to herself that sometimes dreams do come true.

CHAPTER VI

Great Day

THE SURPRISE THAT NAN CONNOR HAD PROMISED TURNED out to be grand indeed. On the three week ends following, each girl flew with experienced stewardesses on observation flights. Vicki's delight was almost matched by that of Celia, who could only gasp, and of Tessa, who went around declaiming scraps of poetry, both appropriate and inappropriate. Jean Cox pretended to be very professional and offhand. Actually she was feverishly excited. Charmion bloomed with work to do, and Dot Crowley tried hard to be meek and mild, with a string tied around her finger as a reminder. Vicki herself quietly floated from hotel to classes and back, eyes shining, saying nothing, and thereby winning a completely undeserved reputation for poise.

Her quiet manner was absolutely misleading, for Vicki's fair head was full of dreams and adventures. Her three trips were wonderful. On the first two she merely tucked herself in a corner and watched the stewardesses perform. They were friendly young women and trusted Vicki, the novice, to do such things as hang away hats and coats, and help dish up the meals. Vicki would willingly have spent the trips standing on her head if that had been asked of her.

The third trip was even better. Vicki played hostess to a planeful of men and women, under the watchful eye of Miss Kramer, the stewardess she and Jean had met on their flight to New York. Vicki had a struggle but, aside from forgetting to serve the rolls and butter with dinner, and aside from bewildering one man with some startling misinformation, she did quite well. Even the pilot praised her. She flew back to New York tired and very happy.

Then along came final examinations. Those examinations were the most difficult Vicki had ever taken. Knowing that a mark of less than ninety-five meant failure did not cheer her or her suffering classmates. And after the examinations were over, there was the awful period of waiting while the papers were being graded. Vicki knew the candidates were being graded too, and just as strictly, on personality and appearance. Vicki began to wonder why she ever had been so foolhardy as to attempt this work. Before her blue eyes swam imaginary papers marked in letters a foot high: TOO YOUNG. IMMATURE. THROW HER OUT.

Somebody suggested going out to the airport, to

kill time while they awaited the verdict. Out of sheer desperation, they went—and out of longing to be around planes.

The day at the airport would have been glorious except for their collective state of mind. Tessa helped a little by acting out her training flights, playing both herself and a dozen passengers simultaneously. Celia wanted to know: If they passed, would that mean they couldn't get married? Charmion devoutly hoped she, a Wilson, would not be airsick. Jean foresaw trouble but remained maddeningly vague. Dot muttered darkly it was a good thing they had saved the salary received while in training. Vicki called a halt to this imminent panic by suggesting that they call on Ruth Benson, the young woman who, with her staff, had hired them.

"Her office is out here at the airport," Vicki said. "We can make it a sort of this-is-either-a-funeral-or-a-celebration call, in case we pass or don't pass. After all, she got us into this. She ought to have a few words of condolence for us while we wait for our marks."

Ruth Benson did have words of encouragement for them. She admitted Vicki's little crowd of six into her private office, and beamed at them out of those brilliant gray eyes.

"Six weeks later, and in the soup," she laughed at them. "Don't worry. You've probably all passed. See here, I pride myself on picking girls who *can* pass. Not a single girl I've approved for training has failed yet. So cheer up." To Vicki she said, "And how's the baby of the class making out?"

Vicki adored the assistant chief stewardess but wished heartily she had not brought up that embarrassing detail. Once out of Miss Benson's office, and feeling gayer, the girls decided to make Vicki pay a forfeit for being the youngest in the class.

"But I can't help being the youngest," Vicki protested. "Speak to the stork."

"The stork is out to lunch," Jean overruled her. "Let's see, now, what does Baby have to do?"

Celia giggled. "Propose to the chief pilot?"

"That's no good; probably every new class has tried that on him," Dot said scornfully. "I beg your pardon, Celia. I mean, it's a good idea but—well, you know—"

Charmion nodded encouragement at Dot, who was trying hard not to burst.

"I know!" Dot cried. "That young copilot Vicki likes, Dean Something, the handsome one who never heard about girls—"

Vicki moaned. "You're too observant."

"You once said, imagine trying to get *him* to bring you flowers—"

"That's it! That's it!" Jean joined in gleefully. "I saw his name posted on that bulletin board we passed. He's at the hangar right now. Vicki has to hunt up Dean Fletcher—"

"And tell him she's a sweet girl graduate who'd just *adore* some flowers!" Tessa finished.

Vicki paled. Charmion tried to rescue her, but the other girls were intent on mischief. Vicki said miserably:

"But where shall I tell him to send or bring the flowers? If we fail, we won't be at the hotel much longer."

Jean Cox finished, "And if we pass, we'll all take an apartment together. The six of us! What do you say?"

There were cries of assent. They gave Vicki advice and a push, and off she went to the hangar; under their power, not her own.

There was Dean Fletcher, talking to a mechanic who sat astride a plane's nose, high above the ground. Dean looked on enviously as if he would like to be poking in an engine himself. Around him swarmed half a dozen mechanics who looked at Vicki appreciatively. Dean Fletcher's glance at Vicki was maddeningly cool.

After some preliminary gulps she managed to say, "May I speak with you privately, please?"

Dean looked amazed but came over and found Vicki a seat on a large crate, away from the mechanics. They sat down together.

Vicki blushed to her ears. "I can't say it."

"Can't be anything so terrible," Dean encouraged her.

Vicki looked into his honest, sympathetic eyes, and

suddenly blurted out the truth. "It's those awful girls. Just because I'm the youngest, they said I have to—get you to—send me some flowers," she finished weakly.

Dean did not laugh. He gave Vicki a stick of chewing gum, took one himself, and said:

"It's a shame to embarrass you like this. Wonder why they picked *me* out, though." He scowled over this with complete unconsciousness of the real reason. "I guess one copilot will do as well as another, and they saw me around. Well, never mind. We'll fool 'em."

"You'll actually send me flowers?" Vicki gulped.

"Certainly I will. I'll bring 'em. What kind?"

"Oh, any old kind will do. But not a potted plant!"

"To me, all flowers are roses."

Vicki said conscientiously, "Roses are pretty expensive. Better not get roses."

Dean leaned his square chin on his hand and gave the matter thought. "Personally, I think flowers are silly. They're pretty and smell good, sure, but they don't last. Couldn't I bring you something more sensible—like a good book on aerodynamics?"

Vicki sighed. Between this thoroughly masculine Dean and the incorrigibly mischievous girls, she foresaw trouble.

"Or a model plane? You could learn something from that," Dean went on. "Or—I have an extra oxygen mask. Be glad to let you have that. You could make good use of it."

Vicki said in a small voice, "I'm afraid it has to be flowers."

Dean assured her he would think of something. They shook hands, boy-fashion. There was liking for Vicki in Dean's face, but only the merest flicker of interest. The one thing that saved Vicki's pride was Dean's thumping her heartily on the shoulder and saying, "Have four brothers but no sisters, so I don't know about flowers and such. But never mind, I'll show up. We'll fool 'em."

"Thank you," Vicki breathed.

"Sure. See you, Vic." He turned back eagerly to his plane.

What went on in the Barr mind after that interview combined mortification, amusement, and gratitude. Dean really was nice, Vicki decided, and friendly, to come to her rescue like this.

Vicki woke up one morning to find Jean and Charmion dancing around the hotel room in glee, waving letters.

"We passed!" they shouted. "You passed too! Of course we opened your letter. Shouldn't have, but we couldn't wait!"

Vicki immediately telephoned the good news to her family. Ginny and her mother said, "Hurray for you!" Professor Barr said, "Well, this satisfies me that you were right, Vicki."

The telephone rang constantly for the next hour, as

the girls talked excitedly from floor to floor. The whole class had passed. As many as could crowd into Vicki and Jean's room came up to celebrate. A cranky old man across the hall complained of the noise. No one remembered to eat breakfast. But they were all so blissful at becoming air stewardesses that nothing else mattered.

"Now the six of us really can take that apartment," Charmion said eagerly.

"Now we get assigned to our runs!" Jean reminded them.

Vicki as usual was not talking but dreaming.

In a delightful daze she went through being fitted for the trim, blue uniform. There was a second and infinitely satisfactory dose of advice from Ruth Benson. Then came beauty day. Like chrysalises about to burst into butterflies, the girls were sent (at Federal's expense) to a top-flight New York beauty salon. There each one received the permanent wave she had been instructed, earlier, not to have. Each girl received individualized attention on coiffure and make-up and posture, to make each girl her loveliest and most natural self. Vicki emerged with her blonde curls piled in a new fashion, and perfume, and—even in the midst of the excitement—free samples for little Ginny. Tomboy Jean was allowed to keep her cropped hair style. Charmion was smartened up and looked happier. They agreed that the most transformed of all was Dot Crowley: correct hair-do and an improved attitude (thanks to Charmion) softened Dot's willful jaw and made her more likable. The most striking, they all agreed, was brunette Tessa; the prettiest, doll-faced Celia. But the loveliest was Vicki—to her intense embarrassment.

They managed an afternoon off for shopping. It was mostly window shopping, up and down Fifth Avenue, and gazing with awe and rapture at the magnificently dressed New York women. Their mouths watered at the ravishing furs and jewels and French hats. But no one would have exchanged the proud blue uniform—emblem of adventure—for anything they saw.

Vicki did fall victim, though, to the allure of some fine purses in a leather goods shop window. They were curiously grained skins, with markings like raised eyebrows, in a rich butterscotch color. She had never seen anything quite like this leather before, and went in to inquire.

"This is ostrich hide," the saleswoman told her, letting Vicki handle a bag. "The hide is imported from Africa. It's not very expensive there, but here in the United States it is very costly indeed. That is because of the high duty the government levies on luxury imports."

The handbag, with its rough eyebrowlike markings, would have cost Vicki several weeks' salary. She left minus the bag, but with an interesting bit of information tucked away in her mind.

The uniforms were ready, Clarence showed up again and dourly took their pictures, Jean had located a largish and not too expensive apartment which she thought the others might like, and, to top it all, Federal Airlines invited the class to attend a graduation ceremony and a luncheon in their honor.

It was quite a party, the girls agreed afterward. All the top officials of the company were on hand to welcome their new stewardesses. There were flowers and music and reporters and the popping flash bulbs of photographers. There were special congratulations for Vicki when Ruth Benson called attention to her as the youngest stewardess on the airline. There was Pete Carmody, hat jammed on the back of his head, gaily interviewing the girls as if they were all his long-lost sweethearts. To Vicki he said:

"Gosh, you're beautiful, and I mean it. Sorry I didn't get around to see you in all these weeks, Vicki. You missed me—I hope?"

Vicki started to be annoyed at his expert line, but could not help smiling. Pete's grin was infectious, and behind his lighthearted banter had as much friendliness as Vicki's own.

"I've been pining away for you, Pete," she assured him. "How could you go off and leave me and the children, you heartless wretch? When we love you so? Why, the twins have been—"

"I know. Teething," he interrupted her. "Never

mind that monkey business. What I want is a date."

"Mr. Carmody!" Vicki satirically fluttered her eye-lashes at him. "This is so sudden."

"Sudden for me, too," he answered gruffly. "You think I'm fooling. Well, I'm not. Yes, yes, I know, you're off on a run, soon, and have no time for dates. But I like you, Vicki Barr, and"—he jammed his funny hat farther back on his head, and his pert face was serious—"I hope to make you like me."

Vicki stared after Pete Carmody as he walked off to his next newspaper interview. She had been so busy with her thoughts of Dean Fletcher that Pete had never occurred to her as a romantic possibility. Yet he was, apparently.

"It's a good thing I'm going to be too busy to think about either of 'em!" Vicki thought. "At least," she amended, "for a while."

Immediately after the graduation luncheon the brand-new stewardesses were handed their assignments and told they were now on call, any minute of the day or night, to go out on runs. Henceforth, no girl could go anywhere—to the movies, to shop, or even to buy a chocolate bar—without leaving word as to where she could be located within half an hour by telephone. Vicki pointed out to the others that this was not so limiting as it sounded: all any of them had to do was telephone back to the hotel (or, soon, the apartment house) switchboard and ask: "Is there a call for me?" In fact, this routine made Vicki feel important.

More important still was her assignment. Vicki had expected that, as a beginner, she would draw something easy, like the brief New York-to-Boston or New York-to-Washington run. Nothing of the sort. New York was to be her home base. But she was assigned to the Fort Worth plane. Since that was a long run, and since no crew was permitted to fly more than eight hours at a stretch, Vicki would fly only to Memphis. There a fresh crew would come aboard for the rest of the flight to Fort Worth.

So her destination was Memphis, Tennessee, with stops at Washington and Nashville. It was a long flight, with tickets at three points to check up on, and a hot meal to serve, and, on night trips, berths to make up. All the girls had drawn difficult assignments, as if Federal intended to test their mettle right from the start. They were appalled, proud, nervous, and—at least Vicki was—secretly pleased.

The assignments did not go into effect immediately, so the six girls had a little time to devote to the apartment Jean had found for them.

It was a furnished apartment, quite attractive, with a living room, two bedrooms, kitchen, and bath. Dot protested at squeezing three girls into a bedroom, but Jean pointed out that all six of them would rarely be at home at once. Besides, Jean demonstrated proudly, there was a convertible sofa in the living room which opened into twin beds: they could even accommodate more than six in an emergency.

"We'll hardly ever use the kitchen, I reckon," Celia giggled. "Someone can sleep in there."

"Sure," said Jean. "That little light in the icebox is just dandy for reading—if you're a midget and if you don't mind the cold."

"I can cook," Tessa said unexpectedly. "Goulash, spaghetti, hamburgers, fudge—"

"Just a minute." Charmion was the one bona fide housewife in their midst. "Some of the older steward-esses gave me a piece of advice. They said the girls in their apartment tried doing their own housekeeping, and the results were fantastic. Because no sooner would they get started acting domestic than off they'd all go on flights, on two minutes' notice. Then, when they'd straggle back, days later, one by one, tired and hungry, maybe at all hours of the night, they came home to a disorderly apartment and an empty icebox and no clean towels, no clean stockings, no nothing. So they hired a maid."

"A what?" the other girls shrieked.

"A housekeeper. Part time," Charmion said firmly. "And pending your approval, I have gone and done likewise. Mrs. Duff!" she called toward the kitchen.

A roly-poly little lady with white hair and rosy complexion came bouncing out of the kitchen. She looked to Vicki like one of the sunnier-natured of the Seven

Dwarfs. Charmion performed introductions and explained that Mrs. Duff had mothered two previous batches of flight stewardesses.

"Nothing ye can do can surprise me." Mrs. Duff twinkled at them. "A houseful of rampaging girls or an empty apartment left helter-skelter, and the telephone ringing fit to drive a body wild—I know, I know."

"Mrs. Duff is an expert on the telephone," Charmion said.

"Indeed, I can hold off your beaus or reel 'em in for ye. Ah, ye mean calls from the airline? I'm canny there. None of *my* girls ever missed a flight, even if I had to pack her kit and go hunting all over the town for her myself."

Mrs. Duff was unanimously elected to stay. Practically at once, tantalizing odors drifted in from the kitchen, clothes miraculously got hung up in closets, a businesslike bulletin board appeared over the telephone, and Mrs. Duff was discovered combing out the tangle in Tessa's abundant dark hair. The roly-poly housekeeper also announced to the six girls that she was their chaperon as well, and no one was foolish enough to object to that.

"The first ones you'll have to chaperon, Mrs. Duff," Dot teased, "are Vicki and Dean Fletcher. Right, Vicki? Isn't this the evening he's due to show up with flowers?"

"S'posing he only sends the flowers, on account of he's shy," Celia said.

"Suppose he never comes!" Tessa exclaimed. "Or forgets!"

Vicki suffered—not too seriously, but she squirmed. Jean and Charmion, on her behalf, countered the others with expert teasing of their own. Vicki could not eat much of Mrs. Duff's excellent dinner. Her anxious pride got tangled up with thoughts of Dean himself.

However, so much went on, even their very first evening in the new apartment, that Vicki's floral wager withered out of everyone's memory but her own. Ruth Benson dropped by to say hello and look over their new place. Clarence and his camera arrived, bearing Pete Carmody's regards, with special regards to Miss Victoria Barr. Mr. and Mrs. Trimble came in, a little apologetic and worried. They had made a special trip from Florida to New York to make sure their Celia had not moved into a den of thieves. Vicki's parents telephoned, to her great delight—except for Ginny's comment. Ginny said, distantly but bland as ever, "Aren't you *even* engaged *yet?*" Two flying friends of Jean's came in. Tessa's brother showed up, bringing three young men, with a small victrola and records. They all danced, and the phone rang and rang, and Mrs. Duff served refreshments. "Ye'll all have to leave at ten o'clock. These are career girls and needs must have their sleep!"

When the doorbell rang again for the umpteenth time, no one paid much attention. Not even Vicki, who was having a fine time. Mrs. Duff ushered in Dean Fletcher.

Vicki stared. It was the first time she had seen Dean out of pilot's uniform or overalls. She had not realized what a handsome boy he was. Dean was carrying— not a corsage—not the dreaded potted plant—but a long florist's box nearly as tall as himself. It was of cellophane, and inside lay all the flowers of late summer. Vicki was overwhelmed.

"Will this do?" Dean whispered in her ear.

"Will it do!" Vicki exclaimed. "It's—it's— Oh, Dean, how generous you are! How very, very kind. And what lovely flowers!"

The other girls gathered around the great shimmering box, admiring especially the roses and the blue larkspur.

"Roses for your cheeks, blue for your eyes," Dean explained to Vicki. "I tried to get yellow chrysanthemums to match your hair, but the mums aren't out yet."

Vicki shook her head. "I didn't realize you could be so romantic. I thought—"

Dean looked embarrassed. "I have a lot to learn about girls. But isn't this a pretty fair start? Dance?"

He swung her into dancing position. Vicki found that she and Dean danced together so naturally that they might have been dancing partners for years. He was rather tall for Vicki, but that merely put her ear within direct range of the copilot's words.

"Can you fly?"

"No."

"Shame on you. You'd better learn."

Vicki gulped. "Maybe I will."

"Will you go up with me someday? I have a little plane of my own."

"Your own plane! Fun! I'd love it. What sort of plane is it?"

Dean smiled proudly. "Just a little red Piper Cub, but she's fast as ——"

"Telephone for you, Vicki!" Charmion called.

It was the airport. "Miss Barr? Report at five tomorrow morning for the six-o'clock run to Memphis. Hangar Eight."

It was also ten o'clock and Mrs. Duff was bouncing through the living room chasing the callers home.

"Shucks," said Vicki to Dean. "Just when we were getting acquainted. But I'd have to get to sleep soon, anyway." She told him excitedly about her assignment.

Dean's steady gaze did not flicker. "Um-hmm."

"You might say it's a nice assignment, or good luck, or something."

"I've already said it with flowers." He picked up his hat. "See you at six A.M. I'm on that run too." He smiled down at her. "When you bring me coffee tomorrow morning, remember I take cream and no sugar. G'night, Vic."

CHAPTER VII

Three Is a Team

SHORTLY AFTER DAWN, VICKI ARRIVED BY CREW CAR AT
the airport. She found the great buildings deserted, except for a few passengers in the echoing lobby and mechanics working about the distant hangars. Out on the
field, planes stood like silver birds in the fresh morning. It was quiet and dreamlike. But this was better
than any dream, Vicki thought. This was the real
thing. This was the beginning of adventure.

She reported to the station manager, in uniform,
overnight kit in hand, trying to appear calm. Then she
walked the long distance across the field, and entered
Hangar 8. For this hour before flight Vicki had much
to do.

There was only a mechanic in Hangar 8, but it was
not lonely in that big place. The great, gleaming
planes, the bright electric lights, the smell of gasoline
and oil steadied Vicki and quieted her nervousness.
She located the ship she was to fly—a flagship—her

own ship—and boarded it. No queen entering her castle could have been prouder than the small, fair girl climbing up alone into "her" immense airliner.

Her first act, and Vicki performed it with due ceremony, was to put her name plate up in the holder.

As she had been taught, Vicki began to go through the plane, filling out the report sheet in her hand. She inspected and reported on the cleanliness of the cabin, the buffet, the washroom, the exterior. She checked to see that blankets, pillows, oxygen kit, service (or medicine) kit, up-to-date magazines, and dozens of other items, were aboard. A man came from the commissary wheeling twenty-one breakfasts, a vat of coffee, dishes and silver in cellophane bags. Vicki went on to test the air conditioning, the lights, and her telephone— the shortest telephone line in the world—from the cabin to the pilot. Everything was perfect so far as she could see, and she hoped she had not overlooked anything. She turned to look proudly again at the sign: Miss V. Barr, *Stewardess*.

"Miss Barr?" It was a messenger. "Here's your manifest from the flight superintendent."

"Thanks." Vicki took and studied her manifest, or passenger list. It included their weights, destinations, information about their luggage, and several fascinating notes:

Mrs. Alice Graham—*first flight*
Miss Jane Smith—*movie actress, incognito. Wishes*

*to remain unrecognized; wishes not to be met
by newspaper reporters.*

Mr. F. F. Hart—*death in family*

Mr. and Mrs. Robert Stoner—*honeymooners*

Michael Green, Jr., *aged eight—traveling alone.
Just recovered from measles.*

Vicki was impressed with the variety and combina-
tion of her passengers. She hoped fervently that she
would do a good job. This first flight was also her first
real test.

She was conscientiously reviewing the main points
Miss Connor had taught them when someone knocked
on the cabin door and called, "Anybody home?"

It was Dean Fletcher, in his uniform with copilot's
insigne. With him was a hearty-looking man, a good
deal older than either Vicki or Dean, also in uniform.

"Vicki, hop down and meet Captain Tom Jordan.
He's our pilot, and captain of the crew."

"Glad to have you aboard, Miss Barr." Captain
Jordan helped her down and shook hands with her.
Vicki liked his quick, friendly smile, his obvious com-
petence, his big-brother treatment of her and Dean.

"Glad to be in your crew, Captain Jordan," Vicki
said.

"Your first flight, Dean tells me. Well, don't be
nervous. You'll do fine—all our girls do. If you have
any troubles, or any questions, just bring 'em to me.

Or Dean here will straighten you out. Three's a team, you know."

Vicki thanked the pilot. She was so anxious to please him, so happy to be working alongside Dean, so excited about her first professional flight, that words deserted her.

Ground crewmen rode up on little cars and hauled the ship out of the hangar, into the brightening daylight, over toward the passenger sheds. The crew followed the plane. Walking across the airfield between her two pilots, dressed like them in flagship blue, Vicki felt an enormous, growing pride. In twenty minutes the vast plane would be in the air, carrying many people many miles—manned by a crew of three—one of them herself. It was something to belong to such a team! She touched the silver wings on her breast pocket and looked up to see both Tom Jordan and Dean grinning at her.

"Happy, Miss Barr?"

"Aye, aye, sir!" Vicki said enthusiastically.

"Now you'll watch us load her."

"Aye, aye, sir," Vicki said blankly.

Loading crews began their work. But the flight crew, along with the passenger agent, were interested in the estimate of how much the air mail, the freight, and the passengers' luggage weighed, and how much weight was allowable for passengers. Their DC-3 must not weigh over twelve tons, loaded. If the freight or mail load was light, Vicki might be able to tuck in an extra passenger, or two or three.

It took quite a long time for the loading crew to heave crates and mail sacks and suitcases aboard, and to arrange them all so that their weight was evenly distributed and so that they would not roll around, back there in the tail. It was fun for Vicki to watch. She stood out there in the wind, beside the ship, with the passengers waiting and watching in the roped-off area. Vicki saw Michael Green, Jr., aged eight, just recovered from the measles, being forcibly held on his side of the ropes.

Men fueled the plane, using hoses attached to a gasoline truck. The pilot showed copilot and stewardess the meteorologist's report: "The airway will be mostly clear and ceiling unlimited over the entire route. The mountain trip will be mostly smooth air and good visibility. A few scattered clouds over lowlands in early morning. Ground temperatures ranging from seventy to eighty during day, prairies; sixty to seventy through mountains." Vicki digested this weather report, anticipating her passengers' questions.

She boarded the plane, patted her cap further over one eye, and took up her station at the plane door.

The passengers came streaming toward her. First up the steps came an elderly lady. Vicki helped her up, and through the steel doorway, and said, "You are Mrs.—?"

"I'm Mrs. Graham."

"Thank you, Mrs. Graham." The first rider. The elderly lady looked excited, her hat already awry. Vicki checked off her name on the manifest. She suggested that Mrs. Graham sit away up front, where the riding would be smoothest. "You can see more up in front, too."

A big man stood at her elbow. "James Letts."

"Mr. Letts." She checked off his name. How would she remember his name?—for she was expected to address her passengers by name. Letts. Lettuce. He had a green tic. Green for lettuce. That made it simple. If only she remembered not to call him Mr. Salad!

Next, a veiled woman in black came up the portable stairway. "Smith. Jane Smith."

Vicki looked at her and started with recognition. She had seen that face magnified on movie screens, dozens of times. But the new stewardess was discreet. She did not flicker an eyelash. "Miss Smith. Thank you."

The honeymooners, the small boy, the bereaved man, and a crowd of others, all passed Vicki, one by one, and entered the cabin. With each, she took a quick look, thought of her own private way to remember the name, and made a hasty guess as to temperament and how to approach that particular passenger. None of them looked like ogres, she decided with a sigh of relief. In fact, they all seemed to be extremely pleasant people. With the last passenger in, the sign

No Smoking—Fasten Your Seat Belt—flashed on, and she found that the passengers had taken seats without any suggestions from the stewardess. Vicki did have to switch Master Green to her own jump seat, at the back of the plane, where she could keep an eye on him. And she tactfully requested one lone man to change places, so that the honeymooners, separated and forlorn, could sit together.

Now Vicki went up and down the aisle, seeing that seat belts were fastened around middles, and offering chewing gum, and advice to swallow. Mrs. Graham looked uneasy. Vicki presented her with a morning newspaper, in which she thankfully hid her face.

Vicki glanced at her wrist watch. One minute before the take-off. Her heart pounded. The passenger agent appeared at the door and handed her the plane pouch, containing the mail, logbook, and express records for the trip. He slammed the door shut, and the steps outside were wheeled away.

One engine turned over, one propeller whirled. Now Captain Jordan gunned another engine, and the plane strained, roared. Vicki sat down in a back seat and fastened the seat belt. The plane accumulated power. Outside on the field she saw the starter raise his arm, drop it. They taxied along the runway, slowly, then faster and faster. The ground dropped away, the glass control tower whizzed past. They were up! Vicki held her breath. She thought she would never, never, so long as she lived, get over the pure, sharp thrill of flying.

Below, New York glimmered silver and misty violet in the early morning sun. But Captain Jordan was waiting for her to report to him. The No SMOKING sign went off. Vicki unfastened her seat belt and made her rather rolling way up the plane aisle, to the pilots' cabin. She unlocked the door, stepped through into a cubicle filled with instruments, shut the door again.

"Hi!" Tom Jordan yelled at her over the noise. "Everything all right?"

She nodded, grinned back proudly at Dean, and handed the pilot the logbook and the manifest. He read with interest the names of the people aboard his ship, and handed the manifest over to Dean. Dean looked very solemn on the job.

"Who's the movie star?" Captain Jordan demanded. "Little old lady scared? Let's see the logbook." The pilot looked up the amount of gasoline and oil in the flagship's tanks. "Look, Fletcher, they gave her a new manifold pressure gauge. Good."

"Coffee, Captain? Breakfast?" Vicki asked. She suddenly remembered that she had forgotten to have breakfast.

"Just coffee, when you get a chance."

"I'll have waffles," Dean said, teasing her.

"And a rose on your tray? Yes, sir."

Serving that breakfast was a revelation to Vicki of

what dangers can lurk in rolls and scrambled eggs. The big problem was to get her planeful fed, and the dishes stowed away out of sight, before they landed in Washington. For the passengers boarding the plane in Washington were not to be served breakfast, and if they saw signs of nourishment, there might be questions and hurt feelings. Vicki earnestly hoped that her present passengers would have swallowed their last bites well before the white buildings hove into view.

She started hastily down the aisle toward the buffet. But the honeymooners stopped her. Could the brand-new Mrs. Stoner have some cotton to stuff in her ears, to relieve the pressure? Stewardess Barr graciously brought her some, and adjusted her chair for her, too. Mr. Letts, with the green tie, asked a question about gasoline capacity. One stout lady had strapped herself in so firmly that she could not move, could not even get the strap undone. The stewardess rescued her, and soothed her with a magazine. The stewardess also answered another passenger's question as to why the pilot doesn't lose his way, when he's up so high he can't see anything below but clouds.

The stewardess also persuaded Michael Green, Jr., aged eight, not to crawl up the aisle on his hands and knees, and pop up at the other passengers to scare them. In addition, the stewardess adjusted the movie star's ventilator while pretending not to recognize her.

Five minutes gone! Five irreplaceable minutes

nearer Washington. Vicki finally got to her miniature kitchen. She set linen and silver on the first trays, popped the precooked frozen food into the thawing oven—then the buzzer sounded. She hastened out into the cabin.

"Oh, never mind, Miss Barr, I found my purse after all. It was tucked in the edge of the seat all along," the woman passenger apologized.

Back in the galley, Vicki tried to hurry. But it was like trying to hurry under water, up here where everything was in motion, where her movements took twice the usual effort, knives and forks danced around, and the plane floor stubbornly refused to co-operate with her feet.

"C'n I help you?" It was the small boy, lounging in the doorway. Just the person Vicki did not need.

"Thanks, no. But how would you like to have a buttered roll? Here."

"Naw. I want coffee."

"And grow up to be a dwarf? I have milk for your size."

"I wanna help you," Michael chanted. He had round, determined eyes and tow hair that stood straight up on end. "And I want coffee."

"All right! All right! You can help me. Er—you can put napkins on these trays."

The little boy happily set to folding the napkins into weird shapes. Vicki, despairing, gripped the first tray and went swaying out into the cabin with it. She was about to offer it to the passenger in the rear seat, the incognito movie star, when the plane suddenly dropped. Coffee jumped up like a geyser and sloshed all over the tray.

She carried the tray back into the buffet, arranged a second tray, and started out once more. Beside the movie star, she bent down, held out the tray, and said pleasantly, "Would you like breakfast?"

"Why, thank you, I would."

Then the actress gave Vicki a long, peculiar stare.

"Is anything wrong?" Vicki faltered. She hastily glanced at the food, chair, ventilator. Everything seemed in good order.

"Oh, no. No," said the actress sourly. "Nothing's wrong—"

Vicki waited, to see what happened next.

"—except that you haven't shown the *slightest sign* of recognizing me! I must be losing my public!"

Vicki assured her that of course she had recognized her, and that the captain and first officer were thrilled to learn she was aboard. The actress looked mollified.

"But of course I don't want to be recognized," the movie star protested. "*No* publicity!" And she put on "for disguise" dark glasses which instantly made her conspicuous.

That little junket, Vicki figured mournfully, had cost her an extra five minutes. She got her small tormentor out of the way by giving him his own tray, and hurried up the other breakfasts. Some of the passengers had not expected this service, and were pleasantly surprised. Vicki felt as if she was playing hostess—playing house in the air. It was fun.

Or it would be fun if only she could do it all faster. She had six more trays to serve. She had not brought coffee to the pilots. She had to collect all the used trays, too. And they were now not far from Washington!

Vicki groaned as she wobbled as fast as she could up and down the aisle. Her passengers looked so pleasant and peaceful—no one dreamed the little stewardess was facing a crisis! That Mr. Letts smiled at her so approvingly—if he only knew! At least Michael Green, Jr., was now sitting contentedly on Mrs. Graham's lap.

Vicki managed—how, she could not have said. But she got breakfast safely, if frantically, within the allotted time.

They landed at Washington for fifteen minutes. Mr. Letts and the stout woman left, and new passengers enplaned. Vicki got them checked off on her manifest, settled them, checked their tickets, and once more the flagship took off.

From Washington until the next stop, Nashville, was a peaceful, interesting morning. It did not take Vicki long to pack away the dishes, wash and count the silver, and leave her little sky kitchen shipshape. Now she had time to visit with the passengers, and with her pilots. Captain Jordan came through the plane to chat with the passengers, and to have a cup of coffee. He patted Vicki on the shoulder and said, "You're doing first rate."

Then Dean came back and talked to Vicki and two men passengers about experimental uses of radar in aeronautics. Vicki wished he had chosen a slightly more romantic subject. But when she saw how his eyes shone, and heard the ardor in the young flier's voice, she realized that this *was* his romance. And, liking Dean, liking flying, she made a real effort to understand his discussion.

"Hope I haven't bored you, Vic," he said, turning to go.

"You couldn't bore me with talk about flying!"

He thanked her with his eyes.

Vicki went up and down the aisle at frequent intervals, seeing that everyone was comfortable, and stopped to chat a little with each passenger.

The bereaved man, Mr. Hart, surprised her by wanting to talk. He was a gray-haired, quiet person who had kept very much to himself on this trip. Vicki would hardly have expected him to choose her, a youngster, as a confidante.

"I've lost my only brother, and I'm going home for the first time in years," he said. "Imagine, I'm going to see the house where I was born, after thirty years away. Forgive me for talking so much, Miss Barr, but I've got to talk to someone—and— Well, sometimes you can talk more freely to a stranger."

"You go right ahead and talk," Vicki said sympathetically.

The man told her a fantastic story. Thirty years before, he and his brother had quarreled over some trifling matter. Bitter and stubborn, he had turned his back on his family, his home town, his whole former life. He had deliberately chosen work that would take him to the ends of the earth: he had been a sailor, and now was a sea captain. All these years he had nursed his bitterness. Only now that his brother was dead, and it was too late to right a wrecked life, did he realize his mistake.

Vicki was touched, and sorry for him. She said goodbye to him, when he got off at Nashville, with all the encouragement she could muster.

Only the final leg of her assignment now, and they would be in Memphis—the end cf the run for Vicki and her crew. In that interval, Vicki learned what went on in a movie star's mind. The woman in black, like Mr. Hart, felt impelled to talk. And she chose the discreet and sympathetic stewardess.

"You think me vain, don't you?" she said in a low voice. The famous face grimaced a little sadly. "Believe me, my dear, when you seemed not to recognize me, I was genuinely frightened. An actor's professional

life is brief, at best. We live in fear of losing the public's interest, for that would be our death. And if you
knew, if you could guess, what a tiresome struggle it
is to retain one's looks! I hate it, I'd like never to put on
make-up again. There's the woman I wish I could be
—there's a really lucky and happy woman—"

She gazed wistfully at the unknown, unimportant,
little bride, sitting there in happiness with her husband.

Even Mrs. Graham afforded a revelation.

When Vicki asked her how she was enjoying her
first flight, the elderly woman replied:

"Shucks, child, this is only my first flight as a *passenger*. Why, I've been barnstorming for ten years. And
I'm seventy years old! Ever hear of Alice Tucker,
Flying Grandma, at all the state fairs? You're looking
at her right now!"

And then they were circling, coming down over the
Memphis airport, to Vicki's disappointment. Her first
trip was over all too soon.

Dean and Captain Jordan, too, would have enjoyed
going on with the plane the rest of the way to Fort
Worth. But they had completed their leg of the flight.
The two pilots and Vicki walked slowly off the airfield,
watching as their flagship was refueled and a fresh
crew prepared to board her.

"How's about lunch, children?" Captain Jordan said.

"And then we'd better go back to our hotels and rest. Have to keep in perfect physical condition. Yes, I know, Vicki. We don't feel tired. But we are. Just wait until you hit your hotel room this afternoon."

The pilot was right. Vicki, in her hotel, closed her eyes "for just the tiniest instant," she promised herself, and awoke only when the telephone rang. The room was dark and Dean's voice, coming out of the receiver, said:

"It's seven P.M. and the captain wishes you at his table."

The three of them spent the evening strolling along the southern streets, talking of flying, and yawning. It was a happy, companionable time. Vicki hungrily breathed in the sweet, close-to-earth air, and realized that her duties in the high, thin atmosphere constituted hard work. But she would gladly ride a rocket to the moon, if necessary, to remain a member of this team!

They worked the trip back next day, starting in the afternoon, and flying straight through to New York without stops. When they landed, New York was a carnival of lights.

Vicki went back to the apartment and slept. Not a soul was there, except comfortable Mrs. Duff. Vicki slept a large part of the next two days, in which she was required to rest before her next flight.

She did, however, go out to the New York airport and hang around the planes. And there she found three communications for her: a photograph of the movie star, cordially autographed to Vicki Barr—a letter addressed to Federal from Mrs. Graham, praising "that nice young stewardess"—and an approving pat on the back from Ruth Benson.

CHAPTER VIII

The Mysterious Mr. Burton

BY SEPTEMBER, VICKI REGARDED HER NEW YORK-TO-
Memphis run with nonchalance. With some pride too,
for she had been transferred from the morning run to
the evening flight. There was a dinner to serve, more
elaborate than lunch, and there were five stops instead
of two. But an evening run had a gala air about it. The
passengers were more relaxed, it was exciting to fly
amid the sunset streaks and then the stars. Even the
airport looked doubly enchanted when one took off at
seven in the evening.

Every seat was taken, this hazy blue evening, as
Vicki's plane cleared the lighted towers of New York
and climbed up to meet the night. The passengers
looked interesting too. Her manifest told her there was
a Brazilian diplomat aboard, whose black fedora hat
she would have spotted anyway; an atomic scientist, a
mild-looking man with glasses; a famous sculptress, a

handsome woman in tweeds. Besides, there were others whom Vicki must remember by name: Mrs. Brown, obligingly dressed in brown. Mr. and Miss Lane— Lane rhymed with *pain*—and suited the sour expression on their faces. Mr. J. G. Burton, going to Memphis, did not rhyme with anything Vicki could think of, as she passed out chewing gum and evening newspapers. Mr. Burton was wearing a gray suit, gray hat, white shirt and black string tie. He was clean-shaven but the bluish shadow of a heavy, dark beard showed. He sat beautifully erect, and held in his hands a bulky brief case of the same ostrich leather she had admired so much in that handbag in the Fifth Avenue shop.

"Ostrich, Burton," Vicki said to herself, entering the galley. "Burton, ostrich. Good posture, Burton."

She giggled softly as her imagination presented her with a flash of one ostrich standing up very straight, and another ostrich slumping and looking ashamed of itself.

Dinner was a scramble. Once out of New York, Vicki started serving immediately. With half the trays served, their plane landed at Philadelphia airport. Vicki had to get the right passengers off, have a moment with the Philadelphia passenger agent to figure weight spread, check new passengers aboard and get them seated, and go right ahead serving dinners. Then she had until the next stop at Baltimore to get the other passengers fed and the culinary evidence stowed away. Besides, there were itineraries to keep track of, for Vicki had to watch that no one rode beyond the point he had paid for. There was the mail, the logbook to carry forward to the pilot, coffee for pilot and co-pilot—who were Messrs. Frane and Tedesco, tonight. The flagship went soaring south through the dusk, and Vicki scampered through her duties as quickly as the thin air and swaying plane would let her.

"Baltimore!"

Circling, seeing the lights at the landing field, coming down softly as a feather. More passengers on and off. A consultation with the Baltimore passenger agent. Baggage, weights, tickets. The hustle of arrival and the sheer exultation of take-off.

"Whew!" said Vicki, once they were up again over Baltimore. "Now I can catch my breath—for a few minutes—I hope!" Most of her passengers would be getting off at Washington.

Mr. John Ogilvie buzzed for the stewardess. Vicki made her way up the aisle, balancing herself with a hand on the high luggage rack. Mr. Ogilvie was stout, elderly, and flirtatious. Vicki awarded him her sweetest professional smile and mentally classified him as Mr. Bore, Mr. Wolf, or both. But it was her job to be pleasant.

"I just wanted to tell you, Miss Barr," he said, beaming, "how much I enjoyed the dinner. At no charge, too."

"I'm glad you liked it, Mr. Ogilvie. Federal makes a point of extra services. I hope you'll ride with us again."

"Well, I'm one who understands good food. One of the few." He harrumphed. "I pride myself on knowing the best restaurants in every city your plane touches."

Vicki opened her blue eyes very wide and looked admiring. She thought of saying that her father shared Mr. Ogilvie's enthusiasm, but it was better manners while traveling to avoid any personal note. So Vicki just looked admiring.

Mr. Ogilvie liked it, apparently. He harrumphed again. "I suppose a charming girl like yourself has many dinner invitations from the passengers?"

Uh-huh, so that was it. Why, he probably had a wife, ten children, and two dozen grandchildren. Mr. Ogilvie was practically the last person in the world Vicki would have wanted to dine with.

"I receive a few invitations now and then. Oh!" Vicki turned her fair head sharply and did a credible imitation of looking alarmed. "The heater! It needs adjusting. You'd be surprised how chilly it can get up here without that heater on, Mr. Ogilvie. Even though it's only September. It gets so cold at this altitude."

"Well, come back and chat with me when you can," Mr. Ogilvie grumbled.

Vicki excused herself, and went off toward the

heater. It was amazing how often that heater needed adjusting. Any time a passenger became too forward, the heater obligingly broke down.

However, the Ogilvies were the exception. When passengers did want to talk with the stewardess, usually it was out of plain lonesomeness. Mrs. Brown, tonight, poured out her worries into Vicki's ear. Vicki finally had to excuse herself, for Mrs. Brown was monopolizing her, and the rest of the passengers expected the stewardess to chat with them a few moments. Or passengers wanted to ask questions about the flight, like this grave atomic scientist, who gently conversed with Vicki about aeronautics as if her erudition matched his own. The only person aboard tonight who did not look up and smile and chat, as Vicki paused beside each chair, was Mr. Burton.

Vicki wished he would talk, for she was fascinated by the rare and handsome ostrich-hide brief case on his lap. She wondered how he had come by it. It was rather bulky, firmly locked, and Vicki imagined she detected a faint Oriental fragrance about it. Perhaps not; perhaps someone sitting near Mr. Burton was wearing perfume. Mr. Burton continued to sit stiffly erect in his seat, staring out the small plane window into darkness, so Vicki did not press her attentions on him.

Captain Frane buzzed Vicki to come up front. This pilot was a tall, lanky, dark man whom she had met only before leaving New York. Now he handed her a report in longhand.

"To the passengers, with my love," he said pleasantly. "Pass it around, will you?"

The passengers enjoyed this message from the pilot. Captain Frane had written: "As we circle over Washington, look down on your right and you'll see the White House and the Capitol. The weather should be good all the way to Memphis. If it seems a little rough over Virginia, that's the tail end of the recent storm in Congress."

Captain Frane was nosing their plane over Washington. The beautiful capital city with its white-domed buildings gleamed at night in its lacework of old trees. Vicki saw the plane's landing wheels come down, saw the powerful landing lights shoot beams ahead. The plane dipped.

The Brazilian diplomat rose in his seat and struggled for his belongings up in the rack, as the plane dipped and circled again. Vicki swayed down the aisle to him.

"Please sit down, Mr. Alvares! Fasten your seat belt for the landing. I'll get your things for you later."

The man staggered, looked preoccupied and impatient.

Vicki racked her brains for the Spanish she had learned in high school. The plane swerved again. "Siéntese Vd., y abrigue su—su—" How the dickens did one say "seat belt" in Spanish? The plane rocked,

Vicki and Señor Alvares all but fell into each other's arms.

"Así!" She desperately pushed him down into the chair and fastened the seat belt around him. Then she ran to her jump seat and strapped in.

"Oh, my goodness," she thought, "I hope I haven't offended him! Diplomat! Snippy stewardess insults proud Latin American! International incident!" And then she realized he might not have understood a word of her Spanish, because his tongue was Portuguese. "He'll just think I *pushed* him!"

Vicki felt no better when, on the ground at Washington, newsmen and photographers crowded the plane door to meet Señor Alvares. They posed the diplomat in the doorway but he looked around for something, beckoned to Vicki.

"Yes, señor!"

He smiled at her, dark eyes and dark face flashing with humor. In perfect English, the diplomat said:

"Come here, Miss V. Barr. I want you in here, too. Weeth a beautiful small girl in the picture, I weel land on the front page."

So he spoke English—and had understood her, after all! Vicki grinned back at him, relieved, complimented, and grateful. She stood beside the diplomat and smiled her best at him, thinking as the flash bulbs popped: "Anything can happen to a flight stewardess! Anything!"

"Joe here weel send you a print, eh, Joe?" The diplomat waved, and disappeared into a waiting limousine.

The Washington passenger agent nudged her, and Vicki dimly recalled that she had other passengers, other duties.

She attended to the routine, and out of the corner of her eye saw Mr. Burton get off the plane. She looked right into his face with its shadow of heavy beard, and murmured, "Only fifteen minutes, sir." Passengers often got off at stops to stroll and stretch their legs and get some fresh air. He was carrying his brief case with him. Mr. Burton headed for the white terminal building. Through its enormous plate-glass front, in the bright lobby lights within, Vicki saw him walking toward the telephones. She made a mental note to see that Mr. Burton was back on board a minute or two before the take-off. If he was not, she would have to ask the passenger agent to hunt him up.

Mr. Burton did not return. Everyone else had come aboard. Vicki grew anxious.

The passenger agent said, "Maybe he's not going to finish out the trip. Maybe he's changed his plans and decided to stay here in Washington."

"But he left his topcoat and gloves on his seat."

"We'll give him two minutes. If he doesn't show up by then—"

"There he is!" And then she added, "I think."

A man in a gray suit, carrying a brief case, hurried across the wide airfield toward their flagship. But this man who strode up the portable steps was not so erect as she remembered him to be. Besides, as he came closer she noticed that his face seemed unusually pale. She stepped into the plane doorway and blocked him, inquiringly holding up her manifest.

"J. G. Burton," he said. "Seat Eight."

She had to step aside then, and let him enter. But surely this was not the same man who had got off the plane!

The passenger agent noticed Vicki's confusion. "What's the matter there?"

Vicki confessed, and asked his advice.

"That's an odd one." The passenger agent frowned. "You'd better find out what's up. It's against the airline's rules for two passengers to ride on the same ticket. How do you know their weight is the same? Besides, it looks bad for you. Negligence."

Vicki's heart sank. The engines turned over, the propellers whirled, dust rose up in the night air. Over the noise Vicki shouted:

"Let's see your list!"

"No time! Get in! I'm going to slam the door!"

There was nothing for it but to duck into the cabin, and do what she could by herself. Ought she to report this to Captain Frane? If anything went wrong, the pilot was supposed to be notified at once.

The balance of the journey, from Washington to Tri-City, and thence to Nashville and Memphis, would be a long dull ride, with the plane pulling into Memphis very late at night. The passengers would doze most of the way, and the pilot would dim the cabin lights.

"I won't be able to find out about Mr. Burton that way!" Vicki thought, troubled. "I'd better walk up and down the aisle as often as I can—study him—"

But Mr. Burton had already gone to sleep, with his gray hat pulled down over his face. He slumped. The other man had not slumped. But then, she argued, any person might slump in his sleep. The brief case he kept firmly tucked under his arm, between himself and the plane wall, as if it was very valuable.

Dozens of times she went up and down the aisle. If the man was aware of her searching eyes, he never stirred.

Sitting back in the plane on her jump seat, in the half-light, Vicki went over and over the meager details she remembered. The same gray suit, white shirt and, yes, even the black string tie. The same ostrich-hide brief case. The questionable posture. The dark-jowled face and the pale face—unless she was mistaken. Voice? He had not spoken to her on the first part of the flight, before Washington. He had not even looked directly at her, but had stared out the window.

"But this man is sloppy," she reasoned, "he dropped his handkerchief, and his shoe lace is undone. The first man was stiff and neat as a pin."

She went up once more and leaned over to pick up the handkerchief. There came to her that faint Oriental fragrance, again! It seemed to come from the direction of the brief case. It *was* the same brief case, then—but she could swear it was not the same man!

Vicki suddenly realized that the two men could have exchanged clothing, or at least have exchanged shirts, ties, and hats. Burton One could have met Burton Two in the washroom of the terminal, during the stop, and exchanged clothing to deceive the stewardess. Yes, that could easily be done; and Burton One had gone into the terminal building and stayed a long time.

But why would two men try to share the same ticket? The matter of time might be a possible reason. Waiting for the next plane out of Washington, after her own plane, would have entailed a delay. Maybe the first Mr. Burton could not go on with the journey, and the second Mr. Burton was completing it for him, without delay. Maybe he had found it simpler just to take the seat, rather than wait for the next Memphis plane, and then maybe not find a vacant seat on it, at that.

"But why the hurry?" Vicki mused. "Even if this man took the next plane, he'd still get into Memphis in the wee hours of the morning. He couldn't do business before nine o'clock."

By 2:30 A.M., circling over Memphis, high on its bluffs above the Mississippi, Vicki's worry had not subsided. But she was too sleepy to think much more

about it. Her only decision was not to bother the pilot
with this doubtful matter.

She saw Mr. Burton drowsily leave the plane. There
was no trace of the heavy shadow of beard that she distinctly remembered. Her suspicions reawakened.

"I'll report it back in New York," Vicki thought, as
she saw the last passenger off and checked through the
empty plane for any forgotten articles. "What that
man, or those men, are up to is surely baffling. It may
be nothing but routine business, after all. I wonder
what—"

The figure of Mr. J. G. Burton, dividing now into
two separate, identically dressed men, now merging
back into one figure, continued to puzzle her.

CHAPTER IX

Troubles

EVERYTHING SEEMED TO BE GOING WRONG FOR VICKI. FOR one thing, she was in trouble about the Burton ticket business.

The very next morning after returning to New York, Vicki went straight to Miss Benson's office at the airport, and reported the matter. Ruth Benson was kind, as always, but her brilliant gray eyes looked sharply at Vicki.

"I'll have to let the superintendent know. And I'll have to report to the ticket department," Miss Benson said.

Vicki stared at the miniature silver and china knick-knacks on her adored "Benny's" desk, and could think of nothing to say.

"Oh dear, Vicki! I wish this hadn't happened! I'm afraid you were negligent."

Vicki hung her ash-blonde head. "I hope this won't

leave a big black smudge on my record. I feel so foolish—but my *record*—I do so want to make good here!"

"Well, don't worry about this. I'll do the best I can for you. Everyone makes mistakes. Next time report things of this sort to the pilot."

Miss Benson's phone rang and Vicki realized it was time to leave. She thanked Miss Benson and went out with dragging feet.

It was only 10:30 in the morning, and raining, a steady fall rain. Vicki had the next two days off, to rest. She did not know what to do with herself. She could go back to the apartment, of course; Jean and Charmion were home now, resting. But she thought she would rather stay around the airport and watch the planes. After trying that for a few minutes, Vicki gave it up. Flights were canceled because flying conditions were not satisfactory. The airstrip was empty, with the rain beating down on it. In the terminal building huddled a few disconsolate travelers, waiting for the rain to stop. Vicki went into the Kitty Hawk Restaurant and had a cup of coffee, hoping to see someone she knew there—hoping to see Dean, she admitted to herself. All Vicki got for her pains was the cup of coffee. She even wished Pete Carmody would show up—at least he was always gay—but the newspapermen had abandoned the airport to the rain.

"Well, I'll leave this soaking, lonesome Long Island,

and go into town," Vicki decided. "After all, I'm in New York, of all wonderful places, and there's lots to see and do. Who's afraid of a little rain?"

She slipped into a telephone booth and called the apartment. Jean answered.

"Hello, ducky, and I do mean 'duck.' We'd given you up for drowned."

"Not drowned, just blue. Indigo, in fact. How would you and Charmion like to go sightseeing with me?"

"In this downpour? What would you suggest, dear —rowing in raincoats in Central Park? A nice swim up and down Fifth Avenue?"

Vicki quavered, "It's dry inside the restaurants and theaters, I'll bet you anything. And if you can stand it, there're museums. Lots and lots of museums. I'm that desperate."

She heard Jean groan and say, "Here, Charmion, she needs that sympathetic Wilson touch."

Charmion's gentler voice came over the telephone. "Now, baby, this is no weather to go tramping around. Besides, we all need to rest. Come home and I'll bundle you up in my nice warm afghan and make you hot chocolate and we'll talk our heads off."

"Yes'm," Vicki said gratefully, and hung up.

On the subway ride home, Vicki felt a little ashamed of herself. If Charmion, with tragedy in her heart, could master her emotions, there was no excuse for Vicki's being moody. After all, this ticket mix-up was not the end of the world, she told herself stoutly. Such things as atomic energy were quite possibly more important. She stopped at a vendor's stand and bought presents: an armful of flowers for Charmion, a magazine on flying for Jean, and a tiny model of the Empire State Building to send to Ginny. But her efforts to feel gayer did not work. She was still troubled about the Burton affair.

Going back to the apartment, to Mrs. Duff's motherly presence, to the warmth of being with Charmion and Jean, was comforting.

"On rainy days, I always fix something specially good to eat," said Mrs. Duff, coming into the living room with a freshly filled cookie jar.

"And turn on all the lamps," Jean said, doing so. "The heck with a few extra pennies on the electric bill. Charge it up to morale."

Charmion said that at least it was a good day for manicures and gossip. She made Vicki lie down on the couch, tucked a soft knitted afghan over her, "and you can even have the flowers at your elbow."

"Makes her look like she's dead," said the forthright Jean. "The helpless type, and look what all it gets her! Golly, I'm going to try being helpless myself. Why so pale and wan, fair damsel? Is that Kelly or Sheets?"

Vicki recited her tale of Mr. or Messrs. Burton. Both her friends pooh-poohed it. "Just snitching a ride, the cheap skates," said Jean. Charmion pointed out that the airline probably would not discharge a stewardess for one error, particularly after having gone to the expense of training her. Mrs. Duff's consolation was more practical: she brought in lunch.

Charmion and Jean chatted on, of the Flying Scouts, a group of teen-age girl pilots, who owned on a share plan, Jean said, a plane and a half. Her younger sister belonged. Vicki tried to prick up her ears on Ginny's behalf—imagine, many of these girls of ten and twelve were already licensed pilots! Ginny might be interested in a flying club for herself and her friends. Vicki listened, too, to Jean and Charmion talk of the women pioneers in aviation. Jean said proudly that she knew the famous Phoebe Omlee, one of the very first American women to fly, and promised to introduce the girls to her one of these days. Charmion's face lit up, but Vicki, still comparatively ignorant of flying, could not fully share their interest. She was still preoccupied with the odd, disturbing events of her recent flight to Memphis.

Late in the afternoon, the telephone rang and woke Vicki out of the nap she had firmly intended not to take. It was Dean Fletcher.

"Are you free this evening, Vic?"

"Yes, unless Federal changes its mind at the last minute. What's on the agenda, Dean? Dancing, please, maybe, I hope?"

"Well—I thought—there's an unusually good lecture tonight on radar—"

Vicki gulped. "I'd love to go. Radar is just what I love most."

"I'll take you dancing afterward," Dean apologized. "I really ought to go hear that lecture. And it wouldn't hurt you, either!"

They agreed on seven-thirty, with Dean to call for her at the apartment, and Vicki hung up.

"A date with Dean?" Jean nodded her cropped head. "That ought to cheer you."

"But a lecture! Gosh, on *radar*. The boy's wooing me with nuts and bolts."

Charmion said sagely, "You ought to be complimented, Vicki. If Dean didn't like you, he wouldn't want you to share his dearest interest." She sighed. "All the times I sat beside Hank in plane sheds and laboratories! I'd sit there until I was cold and stiff and hungry. Hank used to say, 'Honey, if you didn't love flying, I couldn't love you.'"

Vicki and Jean murmured what consolation they could. There was not much anyone could say, except to show Charmion that they loved her.

"Now, Vicki, you better get dressed." Charmion determinedly changed the subject. "You want to look pretty for Dean, don't you? Come on, I'll lend you my new hat."

"It's a fine lecture hat," Jean said. "It will keep the

audience amused when the lecture gets dull. That
hat has a bird on it, and a leg of lamb, and a piece of
an old—"

Charmion smiled. "That's enough. Let's go to work
on Vicki, shall we?"

Vicki was partially beautified, and coiffed in an odd
manner Jean originated, when Mrs. Duff summoned
her to the telephone once more.

"Miss Vicki Barr? This is Peter Carmody. You probably remember me—I'm the one you shooed away.
The one who won't stay shooed."

Vicki had to smile. Pete talked so big and bold to
her that she suspected he was bluffing. "Never heard
of you," she stated.

"I'm the one with the hat," he said earnestly. "Remember the hat? Now try to think of what went under-
neath it. Hair, eyes, nose— Remember?"

"Can't remember a thing," Vicki said firmly.

"Ah, Vicki, it was *me,* all the time," he said with
such plaintiveness that Vicki stopped her teasing.
Pete went on to say that he had just inherited two
seats for the biggest hit show in town, for tonight. "I
know it's short notice, but can you come? Dinner together first. Anywhere you say. I'm rich tonight. I have
an extra dollar."

Vicki was forced to say she already had an engage-
ment, but omitted to say it was for a lecture. She promised Pete to see him soon.

"I may not have theater tickets next time," he warned. "I'm just a poor young newspaperman, struggling along on ideals, stale buns, and old typewriter ribbons. Next time, we might not manage anything fancier than riding back and forth all night on the Staten Island ferry."

"That sounds like perfectly good fun," Vicki replied.

"When there's a moon, and you can see the New York sky line and way out on the Atlantic, it's wonderful. There's an old man on the boat with a hurdy-gurdy. And sea gulls and ships and salt air and stuff. Of course it ain't The Thittr."

"Peter Carmody, I like you and we will go riding soon on the Staten Island ferry. Good-bye," Vicki said, and hung up.

The phone, still under her hand, rang again.

"Vic? Dean. Vic, I'm terribly sorry—don't know how to say this—but, well, you know how it goes. The airline just called me to go out in half an hour on the Norfolk run. Huh? What? So'm I. So long, Vic. See you."

That made everything just perfect. Well, she might as well phone Pete back and accept his date.

Vicki lifted the receiver once more, and dialed his newspaper office. She was informed that Mr. Carmody was somewhere out on his news beat.

"So that is that. Invited on two dates, and left with none." Vicki gave her blonde hair a yank and glared at the phone.

It shrilled again. A woman's voice.

"Miss Vicki Barr? . . . Sorry we have to cancel your two-day rest period, but Stewardess Peggy Crile is out sick. Please report in an hour for the seven P.M. run to Memphis. Flight Twenty-One. Hangar Eight."

This time Vicki shrieked.

"Oh, a stewardess's lot," sang Jean and Charmion to her, "is not a happy one, is not a happy one, is not—"

"Off to Memphis," Vicki said between her teeth. She leaped into her uniform, snatched up her cap and gloves and bags, and ran. Downstairs in the rain, at the curb, a crew car was waiting for her.

Sobering memories of her last flight to Memphis, and of Mr. J. G. Burton, returned. The morning's black mood returned. "Stop it," Vicki said to herself all the way out to the airport. "You mustn't give in to moods." But this was no mere whim. This edginess that possessed her was like a danger signal. As if her nerves were automatically going on the alert, because they sensed some waiting danger.

Why, oh, why couldn't she have stayed in their snug apartment tonight with Jean and Charmion? She had only the briefest visits with them these days. Why did she have to go flying in the rain tonight, worse luck? For that matter, why had she ever been so foolish as to leave The Castle? Homesickness struck Vicki with a thump. There rose up before her eyes, in the rain beyond the windshield, a picture of her father smiling at her over a cookbook—her lively mother, shaking her short curls—Ginny, all braids and glasses and severe expression and love. Even Freckles could have consoled Vicki tonight—except that the spaniel probably would have backed off, as usual, from the perfume she wore. She thought of The Castle as if it were the center of the universe, and heartily wished herself there. The crew car delivered her, instead, to the drenched airfield.

At the airport, Vicki signed her initials on the check-in sheet and darted into the stewardesses' lounge for a moment, for her raincoat and mail. Perhaps there might be a letter from home. But there was no mail at all for her. Ruth Benson was curled up on the sofa, reading a long report. She saw Vicki and called her over.

"The Burton ticket thing?" Vicki asked fearfully.

"No. This is something else. You may be transferred out of New York—Memphis your home base."

"But I don't know a soul in Memphis, Miss Benson!" Vicki wailed. "All my friends are here in New York!"

"There are people in Memphis too," said Miss Benson crossly. "It's only maybe." She went on reading her report.

Vicki ran through the rain to the hangar, gave her plane the preliminary checkup, picked up her manifest, then hunted out her pilot. She found him in the meteorologists' room, studying weather maps. It was Captain Frane again tonight, with a copilot Vicki did not know. Captain Frane told her about flying conditions, and gave her a copy of the flight plan, so Vicki could answer passengers' questions about altitude, speed, and estimated times of arrival. Then they stood out in the wet beside the plane, while the loading crew worked.

The loading crew and passenger agent computed weights, totaled them, and Captain Frane shook his head.

"Someone will have to get off and wait for the next plane. Whoever was the last to buy a ticket is the one. Vicki, this is where you come in."

Vicki went inside to the ticket agent and learned that a Mr. Dudenhoffer was the person who bought the last ticket. Mr. Dudenhoffer, said the smartly uniformed girl with awe, weighed three hundred and ten pounds.

"A substantial gent," said Vicki.

"A solid citizen," the other girl agreed.

Vicki went back to her plane and, in the cabin, identified Mr. Dudenhoffer as that large and ominous-looking man. He was trying, unsuccessfully, to strain the seat belt around his middle, and he was very cross. Vicki was mouse size beside him.

It took a great deal of courage to approach him, explain the situation tactfully, express regrets, and promise a seat on a subsequent plane, and—then!—ask this giant to get off.

"I won't budge," growled Mr. Dudenhoffer.

"But we have no choice, sir. And we're not permitted to take off mail or baggage, as you know."

"Here I am and here I stay!"

"If you don't get off, Mr. Dudenhoffer, you're forcing us to wipe out this trip, and reinstate twenty-one passengers."

"I'm sitting right here!" he bellowed.

Minutes were ticking by, the other passengers fumed, the starter on the field signaled to Vicki that they were late, to hurry up. Vicki pleaded. The angrier Mr. Dudenhoffer got the nicer Vicki became. It did no good.

"If you want me off, you'll have to *carry* me off!"

In the end, that was exactly what it took five men to do. They carried Mr. Dudenhoffer off the ship and dumped him, as courteously as possible, back at the ticket desk.

"I'll get you fired for this!" he thundered at Vicki. As if it was *her* fault!

"Yes, sir," Vicki said sweetly, quaked, and fled.

There was one more delay. Tonight she had a blind passenger, bound for Memphis, coming aboard at the last minute. The man had his big, patient Seeing Eye dog to guide him. Vicki let the dog in the cabin, and left him beside his master's chair. Although animals travel as excess baggage in the cargo bin, a Seeing Eye dog is carried, without cost, in the cabin beside the blind person. Vicki did and said what she could to make the blind man feel safe and secure, then hurried to receive the logbook from the passenger agent.

Her flight certainly was starting off on the wrong foot. Aloft, she had to race to get half the dinner trays served before they came down at Philadelphia. A woman passenger had a bad cold; Vicki stopped to bundle her up in blankets and give her an aspirin. Another passenger wanted to know if they would make up the lost minutes or be later still, since he had other plane connections to make. Vicki had to go up to the pilots' cabin to ask. She relayed this information to the passenger, started back toward her galley, when something caught her eye.

The man reading the newspaper had on his lap an ostrich-hide brief case. It was noticeably like the one Burton had carried. Vicki stood in the aisle, studying it. This brief case, like Burton's, had markings like raised eyebrows, a stout lock, even a similar bulkiness. It was not the same brief case Burton had carried, because this one was a deep shade, and Burton's had been a light shade. But it was twin to Burton's. She was not sure whether she could smell that faint Oriental fragrance or not.

"What's the matter, miss?"

The owner of the brief case had looked up and caught her staring. He was a nondescript man—neat dark suit, a face you could see a thousand of anywhere. His eyes were sharp, and fixed on Vicki.

She had to think fast. She could say something about the Seeing Eye dog, since the dog and the blind passenger were sitting just across the aisle from this man. But the blind man might hear. Besides, Vicki wanted information.

"Sorry to trouble you, sir, but I'm not sure I checked you off on the manifest—what with Mr. Dudenhoffer!" She laughed hollowly. "You're Mr.—?"

"Morris. Charles Morris."

"And your destination, Mr. Morris?"

"Memphis."

"Thank you, sir. I'll bring you your dinner in a few minutes." She smiled and moved away.

Behind that smile, behind that professional poise, Vicki was excited. A similar brief case. The same destination, via the same Washington route. And Morris was following right on the heels of Burton. This might be coincidence, or part of a pattern of events. Vicki determined to keep a close watch tonight. She would be particularly careful to notice whether Mr. Morris—carrying his brief case—went into the terminal building at the Washington stop.

She thought about Mr. Morris all the time she was heating the dinners, and even during the Philadelphia stop. There, two passengers got off, leaving two vacant seats. After they left Philadelphia, the Seeing Eye dog behaved strangely.

Vicki noticed that the dog was restless. She sup-

posed it was because he disliked the motion of the
plane. But several times Vicki saw him rear and snort,
lunging in the direction of that brief case, across the
aisle from him.

"Perfume! Freckles hates perfume! And this dog
smells something in the brief case!" Vicki remembered
the dry, musky scent that had emanated from Burton's
brief case, when she had leaned over to pick up the
sleeping man's dropped handkerchief. It had smelled
like a sweetish talcum. "Same sort of brief case, same
scent—and the scent is bothering the Seeing Eye dog.
Well, I just hope the dog won't annoy Mr. Morris. He's
keeping that brief case on his lap as if he wouldn't
care to part with it."

That was odd, too, holding it locked on his lap. Most
businessmen put their brief cases up in the luggage
rack and forgot about them. Or they opened up their
brief cases and worked on the papers in them. Mr.
Morris did neither, nor had Mr. Burton, Vicki recalled
curiously.

She came out of the buffet after preparing the last
of the dinners. She had yet to serve Mr. Morris, the
blind man, and two others sitting up at the front of the
plane. Vicki was debating if and what she could feed
the dog—poor creature, he must be tantalized by the
warm odors of food, as well as annoyed by that perfume—when she noticed Mr. Morris had changed his
seat. That was probably to separate his brief case from

the irritated dog, Vicki decided. She thought no more about it.

But when she came to serve Mr. Morris his dinner, she found that the brief case was nowhere to be seen. There was no place on the plane to secrete anything. Mr. Morris must be sitting on it. How odd. As if he did not want the dog to draw attention to that brief case again. Vicki was disturbed.

When they came down shortly thereafter at Baltimore, Vicki kept a close eye on him to see if he would get off. But Mr. Morris stayed in the plane.

Later, when they arrived in Washington, Vicki really kept watch.

Mr. Morris walked off the plane, tightly clutching his brief case. Vicki got off the plane too and stood outside it, so she could follow the man with her eyes. He walked rapidly, almost hastily, across the airfield, into the terminal building. He made his way across the brightly lighted lobby toward the telephone booths. Then he must have entered one of them, for she lost him. Vicki kept her eyes peeled, with maddening interruptions from the passenger agent, throughout all fifteen minutes of this stop. Mr. Morris did not come out of the telephone booth—she could not see him moving around anywhere in the lobby— Unless she had missed him—it was hard to pick out one figure in a crowd.

They had refueled, Vicki had checked new passengers aboard, the fifteen minutes were up. Mr. Morris had not returned to the plane. Vicki notified the passenger agent.

"I'll send someone to look for him. Dark-blue suit, yellow brief case, right? Okay."

They held up the take-off for two minutes. The search produced no sign of Mr. Morris.

"Let it go," the passenger agent told Vicki. "Looks like he decided not to ride out the rest of the trip. Maybe he'll finish it out on a later plane."

It looked to Vicki as though Mr. Morris did not want to finish out the trip on *this* plane. Not with the Seeing Eye dog aboard to call attention to his brief case. *What was in that brief case?*

Vicki reported the whole disturbing affair to Captain Frane, at the weary end of the run. The pilot agreed that the circumstances certainly looked suspicious, but that there actually were no grounds on which to take action. He cautioned Vicki that if Morris ever appeared on one of their flights again, she was to advise the pilot immediately.

CHAPTER X

The Night Run

A MONTH WENT BY, AND NOTHING HAPPENED. AT LEAST, nothing happened on the Burton-Morris mystery, and Vicki considered anything else secondary. Actually, a great deal did happen. The calendar moved from September to October, the girls changed into their winter uniforms and carried topcoats. They were all steadily gaining in poise. In her free time, Vicki was dragged to two lectures by Dean, and she attended a party with Pete Carmody—it was too chilly by this time to ride the ferryboat. Letters came from home, describing the changing season in the garden, and the reluctance of Ginny's return to school. Letters came from passengers, saying "Miss Barr was so nice, and am enclosing a hat [or alarm clock—thermometer—desk set—salt shaker] as manufactured by my company." Time and planes flew on, and so did Vicki. Every day brought her new, bewildering, hilarious assortments of passengers and situations.

These were busy days for Vicki, yet she was never so busy as to forget completely the men with the ostrich-hide brief cases. She was surprised at herself for worrying so, and for taking the incident so seriously. On every flight she half looked for a man with a telltale brief case. She supposed that, with a month gone by, she might as well give up looking.

Then one night Vicki finished her run at Memphis. It was two-thirty in the morning when they landed. Captain Jordan and Dean were her crew tonight. The three of them stood on the dark, windy airfield, in the slanting glare of beacon lights. They watched the fresh crew take over the plane, to fly her on to Fort Worth, and felt a little envious as usual. Then they drove on to their hotel, tired, eager for sleep.

Downtown Memphis was deserted and dark, except for a few lighted store fronts and all-night restaurants. Even the lamps in the lobby of their hotel were dimmed. They spoke softly to the night clerk and registered. The only other person in sight was the night porter, rolling back rugs and mopping up the marble floors.

All this was ordinary enough, yet Vicki never entered Memphis without remembering Burton and Morris. Whatever they were doing was centered right here in this town. She puzzled over it while Dean and Captain Jordan spoke to the night clerk.

A telephone rang, shrill in the night. The desk clerk called softly to the switchboard operator:

"Is that a New York call? We have a guest who's taking an early morning plane and so has checked out of his room. He told me he is expecting a long-distance call."

The operator called back softly, "Yes, this is New York."

Suddenly, out of an enormous wing chair standing in shadow, a man arose.

"Thanks, then that call's for me," he said, and strode rapidly across the wet marble floor, heels tapping. He walked very erect, his movements precise, his posture perfect. A brief case was under his arm—an ostrich-hide brief case. Vicki looked at the dark-jowled face, started. He was the first Mr. Burton!

She saw the man enter the small, adjoining telephone room. The night switchboard operator handed him a phone, then clicked the call off her earphones so that she would not hear his conversation. Vicki heard him say, "Hello . . . Yes . . . Right . . ."

Then Captain Jordan put his hand on her arm. "Come on, Vicki. What are you staring at?"

"That man. He was one of our passengers." She strained to hear his conversation but could not. It occurred to her that by taking the call down here, Mr. Burton—if that was really his name—was making sure the hotel operator did not listen in. If he had taken it in his room, he might have been overheard.

"Vic. Hey, Vic." Dean nudged her. "Are you going

to sleep standing up, here in the lobby? Like a horse?"

"Dean, I—I— Wait a moment." She turned to Dean. He saw the distress in her face and his expression changed. "Stay with me a few minutes," she breathed.

"Sure."

She did not want to let the brief case disappear from under her eyes a third time. Captain Jordan again said, "Let's go," and handed them their room keys.

Dean said, "I think, sir, if you don't mind, Vic and I will run out and get a bite to eat."

Captain Jordan frowned. "I don't like to have you two kids wandering around at this hour of the night. Well, make it quick. I want you both back in your rooms in short order, understand? I'm going to phone you both, and see."

"Yes, Captain Jordan," Vicki said quickly. "Thank you. We'll be back soon, honestly."

Out of the corner of her eye Vicki saw Mr. Burton leaving the telephone room—walking stiffly and rapidly across the lobby—and out of the hotel!

"Come on!" she whispered to Dean. "That man— we're going to follow him!"

"But why?"

"Tell you later," she said under her breath. "Come on!" They fairly ran to the revolving doors.

Out on the street, Mr. Burton was already a diminishing figure at the end of the shadowy block. They sprinted after him.

"He certainly avoided us in the hotel," Vicki thought. Why? It suddenly struck her that he had recognized her. The second Burton—and Morris—must have noticed that the small blonde stewardess had observed them with curiosity. They knew, too, that the first Mr. Burton had ridden on that stewardess's plane and been observed by her—remembered by her—particularly after that ticket trick. They probably had tipped off the first Mr. Burton to steer clear of Vicki.

"And I'm so easy to recognize," Vicki mourned, "with this blue flight uniform and my hair!"

The man with the brief case certainly was taking a roundabout course. He must realize she was trailing him, and was dodging her. He turned corners again and again, through the darkened sleeping city. Twice Vicki and Dean nearly lost sight of him.

Dean asked no questions. He towered above Vicki, who half ran to keep pace with him. She said nothing to Dean for the moment. She was busy with her thoughts.

She recalled a conversation with Jean which had taken place a month ago. Vicki had just returned to New York after the Memphis flight with Mr. Morris and the Seeing Eye dog aboard. Jean had followed home on Vicki's heels. Jean, too, was returning from the New York-Washington-Memphis run, on the plane scheduled right after Vicki's. Vicki had left New

York that evening several hours before Jean did, stopped at Washington, and arrived in Memphis at 2:30 A.M. Jean's plane had left New York late that same night, touched Washington, and landed in Memphis at 5:30, at dawn.

"Quite a run," Jean had agreed. "Glad I didn't have to serve hot dinners as you did. I just gave 'em a cold snack. Oh, Vicki! Remember that ostrich-hide hand-bag you admired so much in the shop? The one with the funny markings you said looked like raised eye-brows?"

"Yes, I remember."

"Well, there was a man aboard my plane last night carrying the most fabulous brief case, made out of that gorgeous stuff! He got on at Washington. I thought you'd be interested."

Vicki had been more interested than Jean knew. "Do you recall his name?"

"Morton? Morris? It was Morris. He was going to Memphis."

So Vicki had learned that Mr. Morris—the third man she had seen in this ostensible chain—*had* completed his trip to Memphis, on the very next plane out. He *had* got off her plane to avoid the dog's attention— and to avoid the too-observant stewardess.

Vicki recalled another thing. On that first trip, when Burton Two took Burton One's seat, rather than wait for the next plane, she had speculated on their obvious hurry. She had wondered what difference it could make to a businessman whether he arrived at 2:30 A.M. or at 5:30. For Vicki had assumed that he could not do business before nine o'clock in the morning, anyway. Now she suspected, with the first Mr. Burton darting down shadowy streets ahead of her, that this might be uncommon business, secret or hurried or both, transacted in the dead of night.

"Cold? Tired?" Dean was looking down at her.

"Neither, thanks. Do you mind this, Dean? It's important—believe me— We mustn't lose him!"

He had led them out onto a high street, from whence they had a night glimpse of the Mississippi, and Memphis's two big bridges. It was an obscure street, dingy, with poor houses with tall stoops and ordinary shops. A light still burned dimly in a jeweler's window, showing his wares, and at the corner an all-night coffee shop was brightly lighted. All else was darkness, and somewhere in the murky doorways, alleys, and turnings, Vicki lost sight of the man with the brief case.

Up and down, she and Dean searched. The man was gone. Vicki and Dean stood looking at each other in the street, forlorn and baffled.

"Did you see where he went?" she asked Dean anxiously.

"No, I didn't. But I don't think he went into any of the houses, because we'd have seen him going up the steps. And I don't think he turned a corner, because there are lampposts at the corners and we would have seen him."

"What do you think, then?"

"I think," Dean said, "that he must have slipped into one of these stores, which have their entrances at sidewalk level—unlike the houses, you see. Or else he ducked down an alley, an alley between either stores or houses."

"I'm not going down any of these black, evil-looking alleys," Vicki said, shivering.

"I don't think it would be wise. Want to see if he's in the coffee shop?"

They were not at all surprised to find he was not there.

"The jewelry shop is the only other place with a light."

"That doesn't mean anyone's there. Shopkeepers leave lights on all night to advertise their wares, or to make it harder for burglars to break in," Dean pointed out.

"Let's have a look, anyway."

They strolled to the middle of the block and peered in at the jewelry shop door. The small store was deserted, with only one small light burning in the window. Vicki looked at the jewelry displayed. It was ordinary stuff, nothing valuable. Just the night display of a poor shop in a poor neighborhood.

"Looks like we've gone on a wild-goose chase," Vicki admitted.

They walked back to the hotel, Vicki in low spirits. On the way, she told Dean the story—told him as her friend, and told him as copilot, in case another doubtful passenger with an ostrich-hide brief case should ever appear on one of his planes. The sky was growing lighter.

"Too bad we lost him," Dean said.

"I'm afraid we didn't learn anything. Just the same—"

"What, Vic?"

"Did you notice the name of that street?"

"Yes, I did. Chickasaw Street."

"Chickasaw Street," she repeated slowly. "I'll remember that."

CHAPTER XI

Going to a Party

"IF YOU WERE ONE YEAR OLD," CELIA ASKED, "WOULD you be insulted at being called Stinky?"

Vicki grinned and reached for another bonbon. "Why?"

"Because," Celia answered gravely, "I could swear one of my passengers didn't like it. At least, he didn't like the patronizing tone of voice."

Dot Crowley said from the depths of the sofa, "Maybe he was a horrible baby and richly earned the name. Barr, will you stop eating candy? You're the only one of us who can do it without getting overweight and being taken off runs. You're torturing us."

"Where do you put all the food?" Tessa asked jealously. "Me, I work like a horse and have to eat like a bird." She stretched out her hand and admired the manicure she was doing.

"I have hollow legs," said Vicki. "Mm, delicious bon-

bons. Especially the pink ones. Such a shame you can't—"

Charmion came into the living room and squeezed into the big lounge chair with Vicki. "Button me up the back, dear, will you? Who's Stinky?"

"Stinky," Celia explained, "is a baby. You know, formulas, pillows, diapers. All you do is pull three corners and put a pin in."

"A pin *in* the baby?" Jean inquired, poker-faced.

"Not unless the plane bumps," Celia answered. She could not understand why they all laughed. "I like babies," the pretty girl said stoutly. "I'm going to ask if I can't be the stewardess on the special baby plane Federal is going to run."

Dot teased: "Why don't you give up your career and get married and raise your own?"

"I would if somebody nice would ask me," Celia said candidly.

"Our Big Executive doesn't understand marriage," Tessa remarked. "She never heard of love. She'd rather have a desk with three telephones than a husband."

"And you'd rather pose in the plane doorway for the photogs, instead of going about your job!" Dot retorted. "Oh, I've seen you, you would-be Katharine Cornell! If you aren't the hammiest—"

The other girls quickly drowned them out, and then the telephone started to ring. They all shrank in their places, dreading a summons to emergency work.

"Someone go," Vicki said helpfully to the room in

general. "Ol' Vicki plumb wore out, needs her rest."

"You go, you've had a light schedule," Jean said to Celia. "Work, work, work!"

"Not me," Celia begged off. "Tessa, couldn't you answer?"

"I should say not! I just gave two of my 'free' days to publicity assignments. Tell the office I'm dead or something."

Tessa glared at Dot. Dot stared out the window. The phone rang on. Charmion climbed out of the chair beside Vicki, making a face.

"I suppose it's up to grandma, as usual. . . . Hello! . . . Yes, sir. Yes, we're all here." Her tone changed, lightened. "Oh, a *party!* That's wonderful. Oh, yes, we certainly are all here!"

Charmion said thanks and hung up.

"The company is giving a big, super-de luxe party, this Sunday, for all the pilots and stewardesses. We're all invited. What shall we wear? Heavens, I haven't anything nice enough for a party!"

Vicki and Jean exchanged satisfied glances. When Charmion, after her emotional seclusion, began to take an interest in going to parties, that was a healthy sign.

"I will wear my purple velvet with the train," Vicki said grandly. She rose and swept around the room, her imaginary train looped over one low-held wrist. "And my ermine cape. And dear, dear, great-great-grandmother's paste tiara."

They all giggled except Tessa, who said wistfully:

"I wore a gorgeous costume like that once in a play. Except that it had no train, and was green instead of purple, and no furs or tiara, and it was a little tight on me."

"Just the same, only different," Dot observed.

"It was gorgeous all the same! I wish I had it now to wear to the party Sunday!"

"To startle the natives?"

"Dot! Tessa!"

"Shucks, I get tired of being tactful," Dot sighed. "I smile on the job till my jaws ache. Can't a girl relax at home and be her own nasty self?"

Dot meant it to be funny, but the others were thoughtfully silent. Then they warned Dot again. "Someday you're going to smart aleck yourself right out of your job, Red. Less push, more tact—*puh-lease!*"

The reception was held at a hotel, complete with crystal chandeliers, orchestra, flowers, harassed waiters, and a long line of company officials to be braved at the door. It was one of those big crushes where an immense ballroom is so crowded that you can't see your own feet—where talk, music, shuffling shoes, and clattering forks equal bedlam fortissimo—and where, if the human surge washes you up against someone you know, you feel like Stanley finally locating Livingstone in the wilds of Africa.

Vicki found Dean, who was towering over everyone

else, helpless with an empty plate in his hand. He was miles from anywhere to set it down. Then Pete found Vicki, who by this time was stuck with two plates, hers and Dean's. Pete had a plate of his own, wrapped in a napkin and nonchalantly protruding from his bosom.

"I got tired of lugging the danged plate," Pete explained. "Easier to carry it. But I thought, if I can shoot myself a waiter on the wing, I'll have a plate for the spoils."

"What do you do with a plate, anyway?" Dean asked wearily. "The best disposal I could think of was to step on it. The hotel wouldn't like that. The next best thing was Vicki, here."

"So I'm a next best! Well, I like that!" Vicki protested. "Wearing my best black velvet dress and bonnet, and I'm a second-best disposal system for dirty dishes."

"He doesn't appreciate you," Pete put in quickly. "Give me those plates, my young lady. I'll get rid of 'em for you later. By the way, introduce this churl."

Dean flushed ever so slightly. Vicki was sorry Pete had chided him. Dean was not really rude, only preoccupied, as always. Pete evidently recognized Dean as competition, Vicki thought, as she introduced the two young men. They scowled at each other and spoke polite phrases.

"This reception is wearing down Mrs. Carmody's little boy," Pete said, balancing the three plates. "My idea of a nice party is to get together five or six people you really like, and play victrola records, and dance, and play games, and broil hamburgers, and the heck with these mob scenes."

"Sounds nice," said Dean. "Am I invited?"

"You are not," said Pete pleasantly.

Vicki put in, "You couldn't be invited, Dean, because it's only a hypothetical party. A beautiful dream."

"Oh, I don't know about that," said Pete. "I have a grand little apartment for giving parties, down in Greenwich Village. Of course, there aren't enough chairs to go around, so you have to sit on the floor, and the decorations aren't by Chippendale, and the landlady howls after we've played boogie-woogie records for two or three hours. Bernard Shaw howls, too."

"Who?" asked Vicki and Dean, blinking.

"Bernard Shaw, my pet monkey. A little tiny brown one. Chatters all the time. You'll have to come down and meet him, Miss Barr."

Dean's face grew long and bitter. "She's already met the monkey," the flier said, and glanced unmistakably at Pete.

Vicki was astonished, and wanted to say, "Well, well! One up for you, Dean," but she had another surprise, a pleasant one, when Pete merely burst out laughing.

"Fletcher, you're the first flier I've met who isn't *entirely* illiterate and tongue-tied."

"Not words, but deeds," Dean mumbled angrily.

"A writer's words *are* his deeds," Pete defended himself. "I may not be a big muscle-and-monkey wrench boy, but I—"

"Truce, truce!" Vicki cried. She seized Pete's white napkin and waved it. "I'm appalled at you both. Shake hands like little gentlemen now."

The flier and the newsman did not exactly kiss and make up, but peace returned. A few seconds later Pete had to worm his way through the crowd to interview a celebrated aerial somebody-or-other who had just come in.

"What do you see in that—" Dean started, but his words were drowned out under the sudden fizzle and pop of flash bulbs. Vicki was spared the embarrassment of answering. Clarence spotted her, and motioned her over to the dais, for a picture with the rest of the stewardesses.

As she smoothed her dress, and went to stand between Charmion and Dot, she shook her fair head a little over the Fletcher-Carmody clash. "I don't want to take sides," Vicki decided. "Don't see why I can't like them both."

"Cantcha look up?" Clarence bawled.

She looked up into his bony, mournful face. "Me?" Vicki smiled radiantly. "How's that for a free sample?"

"Aw right, aw right. Dames! Someday I'm gonna retire and never photograph nothing but dogs and cats."

"Be careful they don't bite you and vice versa," Dot threw at him.

The other girls hastily nudged her, and they all smiled like angels.

Vicki was concerned about Charmion. After Clarence had taken their pictures, Vicki sought out Jean.

"How's Charmion doing? Have you had a chance to notice?" Vicki realized it was no easy thing for a flier's widow to face a crowd of fliers, some of whom Charmion must have known when Hank was alive. Probably some of them were talking to her about Hank. It must bring the memories surging back.

"No, I don't know." Jean was troubled, too. "Let's find her, shall we? Without being obvious about it, of course."

Vicki giggled. "Sure. You're about as secret as long underwear on a clothesline."

"Isn't that Charmion over there?"

They threaded their way over to the tall, fair girl. She was deep in conversation with four men. The men had fliers' wind-burned faces and athletic carriage.

Their talk was far too technical for Vicki to understand. She turned to Jean for help, but Jean was already absorbed, listening with delight.

"I've got to learn more about flying, that's all there is to it," Vicki thought. "If it can make their faces shine like that, I must be missing out on something awfully good!"

Then she heard the gayest of the men refer to Hank. Charmion paled, but looked steadily into the flier's eyes.

"He was a great airman. I know, I worked with him. One of the best of the army pilots, and one of the greatest test pilots we've ever seen."

"Or ever will see," said the oldest man in the circle. "Hank made flying safer for thousands of people. He made an enduring contribution to aviation, Mrs. Wilson."

"Thank you," said Charmion. Her eyes shone for a second with tears. "I'm flying because I think that's what my husband would want me to do."

"Yes, that's what Hank would want," the men agreed. "You're doing the right thing, Mrs. Wilson. Carry on his name in aviation."

"I will," said Charmion. She smiled and added, "It's been good to talk to his friends about him."

She turned away then and saw Vicki and Jean waiting for her. "Oh, here you are. I was wondering if we couldn't go home now. I'm so weary—all of a sudden—" She pressed her hands to her eyes.

Vicki and Jean went home with Charmion. Meeting Hank's friends at the party had been a strain for her, and the gentle girl was exhausted. For a time after that, Charmion was subdued, and sat alone, but presently the salutary effect of facing the situation head on began to show. Charmion seemed to grow relieved, serene, not happier but closer to peace than the girls had yet seen her.

Vicki herself was not feeling in a particularly peaceful frame of mind. In all these days and weeks there had been no further sign of a man with an ostrich-hide brief case. On every run she had watched for him. On every layover in Memphis she had taken walks which ended, invariably and fruitlessly, in Chickasaw Street.

Now, to make her efforts even more hopeless, routes had been changed, and Vicki had just been transferred to the New York-Detroit-Chicago run. She would make no more flights to Memphis, no more stops at Washington. She grasped her ash-blonde locks into a mustache and despaired of ever being on the trail of that mystery again.

"Silly," Jean Cox scoffed. "*I'm* still on the Memphis run."

"But what good does that do me?" Vicki sighed.

"Don't you know we're permitted to swap routes? Brand-new ruling."

"We are! Well, boil me down and pour me out! Will you trade with me, Jean?"

"For you, my love, yes. Glad to. We'll just speak to Miss Benson about it."

Vicki could hardly wait.

CHAPTER XII

The Fourth Man

THE SWAP WAS APPROVED, AND ONE FRIDAY EVENING IN
October Vicki found herself on the plane going to
Memphis.

She thought the fates must be amusing themselves
at her expense—for here on her plane tonight sat a
man with an ostrich-hide brief case. A tall, thin, gray-
haired man whom she had never seen before. The
manifest said: John Neff; destination, Memphis; no
luggage. But he did have luggage—locked and bulky,
held guardedly on his lap, and giving off that faint,
powdery, Oriental fragrance.

Vicki was so flustered she could hardly go about
her duties. It was all she could do to drive herself into
the buffet and start the routine of dinner trays. Her
hands trembled so, in her excitement, that she was
awkward and slow with the work. She served all too
few trays before the plane came down at Philadelphia.

And—oh, what an oversight!—she had forgotten to bring the pilot the logbook.

She hastened up forward, regretting that the pilot tonight was neither Jordan nor Frane. Those two already knew of the mysterious brief case. Tonight's new pilot would be too busy to listen to a wild tale which she knew would sound implausible. She had better not mention the matter to a pilot who did not know her, unless something happened to make it necessary.

The pilot's name was Jackson, and he was annoyed with Vicki for being so tardy with the logbook.

"Sorry, Captain Jackson. Coffee?"

"No," he growled. "You, Joe?"

The copilot, whom Vicki had seen only for a moment at the reception, thanked her and declined coffee.

"Darn it," Vicki thought, back in her sky kitchen once more. "Why couldn't it be Tom Jordan or my nice Captain Frane, tonight of all nights? And what wouldn't I give to have Dean aboard!"

As her hands worked with the food, her thoughts went out to Dean. Strange the way she had been so romantic and excited over him in the beginning—and now, in the brief time since they were crewmates, she could be quite calm over the young airman. She supposed it was because of working together: there simply was not time, nor the right mood, to be romantic on a demanding job.

Still, on the two- and three-day rests in New York, when they had time and freedom for dates, her heart had thumped satisfactorily in his presence. That pulse of excitement did beat on: only work held it in restraint, sometimes. She remembered his long stride, his sinewy face and hands, his serious gray eyes. She remembered dancing with Dean, her cheek on his shoulder, when the world fell away and there were only the two of them, circling and turning and drifting.

"No, I haven't got over Dean," she thought. "Perhaps that certain feeling has even been growing when I wasn't looking. But what a time for me to be thinking these things!" She sighed, and picked up another tray. "I guess it's because I need Dean with me, so very much, tonight. He'd help me . . ."

"Dinner, Mrs. Farber?" she said aloud. "Yes, it is a little rough tonight. But I think it would steady you if you would eat your dinner as usual. Why don't you omit the liquids—the broth and the coffee? . . . Certainly, I'll take them away. . . . Not at all, Mrs. Farber."

She wished John Neff was sitting at the back of the plane, instead of up front. The rule was first to serve the passengers at the back, nearest the galley, and work her way up forward, so no hungry passenger would be tantalized by the sight of trays going past him. Good psychology, Vicki knew, but it meant she had to serve a great many more trays before she could bend over Mr. Neff, up front, offering his tray, and at that moment get a good look at his brief case.

Vicki very much wanted a close look. She had to be absolutely sure it was a similar brief case. If she could invent an errand that would take her up to the front of the cabin— Oh, good. Someone in Seat 2 was buzzing for her. Neff was in Seat 3.

"Yes, sir?" Vicki said to the passenger in Seat 2. She stood squarely in the middle of the aisle, right between Seats 2 and 3, where she could see.

"I wonder if you'd help me read this air map," said the man in Seat 2. "I'd like to follow our course."

"Certainly," Vicki said, and briefly discussed tonight's winds and flying speeds with the interested passenger. She was surprised at how coherent she sounded, for her eyes kept straying to Neff across the aisle. She could not get a good look at his case. He had put his hat on it.

"He saw me looking at the brief case," she realized. "Maybe the other men told him about me."

She decided against speaking to the tall, gray-haired man, much as she was tempted to. She could not afford to rouse his suspicions against her. Back to her miniature kitchen she went.

As she hurried to get dinner over before the Baltimore stop, her brain pieced together what bits of facts she had. Four men so far. All with similar brief cases. That looked like a ring of men, all doing the same thing. All flying the same, fixed itinerary. All starting from New York. All getting in to Memphis well before dawn. That pointed to New York and Memphis as key points, possibly headquarters, and to some need for secrecy and hurry.

"Who is *this* man?" Vicki speculated as she arranged Neff's tray. "He's older and more important looking than the three who preceded him," she mused. "He has a harder face. What's his part in the chain?"

All through her thoughts ran a caution from her conscience. It prodded: "You ought to report this matter to the pilot. Simply to protect the airline. The first two men broke the rule on seats and fares. Morris behaved suspiciously. No telling what this fourth man may have in mind!"

Vicki started up the aisle, balancing Neff's tray, her heart pounding. As she came to his chair, it cost her a big effort to give him his dinner without comment.

"Oh, thanks," he said.

She smiled mutely, not trusting herself to speak.

He put out his right hand to take up a fork, and for the first time, Vicki saw the ring on his finger. It took her breath away. It was an enormous blood-red ruby. The ruby was of such beauty and such depth of color that there was no doubt it was a real jewel.

"Whatever these men do for a living, it must pay well!"

She served the last two dinners, to Seats 1 and 2, in

a daze. She ought to tell the pilot. She ought to report, even if it was a vague report.

Vicki unlocked the pilot's door and stepped through. She blinked in the half-shadowed cabin, with its myriad tiny lights reflected off the black-and-white instrument panels.

"I have something to report, sir."

"Make it short, Vicki. We're busy with this fog."

"It's this, Captain Jackson—" Vicki told him as rapidly as possible about the two Burtons and about Charles Morris. "Now there's a fourth man aboard tonight with an identical brief case."

Jackson looked disbelieving but he listened closely. Frowning, he said:

"Are you positive it's the same kind of brief case?"

She reflected, tugging at an ash-blonde strand of hair. "Not absolutely sure," she admitted.

"Well, go verify it," the pilot grunted.

"You mean I—I'm to go right up to that man?"

"Make an excuse. And hurry up about it, because we're coming into Baltimore in a few minutes."

Vicki stepped back through the pilot's steel door, closed and locked it, and put the key back in her uniform pocket. She made these actions last as long as possible, because only three paces from her sat Neff. The brief case now was tucked in the chair beside him, as he ate with the tray on his lap. She swallowed hard, and on feet of lead went over to him.

She bent over him and cold gray eyes looked up at her instantly.

"Wouldn't you like me to put this on the luggage rack? Up here with your hat?" Her hands closed over the bulky brief case. Her eyes memorized unmistakably the lock, the curious hide, and her nostrils quivered at the powdery scent. "So much more comfortable to have it out of the way, while you're—"

"No!" He caught himself. "No, thanks."

"Sorry, Mr.—sir. Have you finished your dinner? I'll take your tray."

He looked at her suspiciously. Then apparently he, too, decided to play it safe and disarming. "Yes, I've finished, Miss—Miss Barr, I see by the name plate." He smiled. It was like a crack in ice.

Vicki smiled too, the mouse grinning at the cat, and removed his tray.

The plane was circling over Baltimore when Vicki strolled again to Mr. Neff's end of the plane. She managed one more look at the brief case, as the pilot had instructed. Then, for the next ten minutes, passengers disembarking, new passengers enplaning, and a conference with the Baltimore passenger agent kept her busy.

Finally they took off again, and she had a chance to report to the pilot. She had to pass Neff once more. She knew he was watching as she unlocked the pilot's door.

Captain Jackson was too busy clearing the rooftops of Baltimore to speak to her immediately.

"Yes?" he said finally.

"It's the same kind of brief case. I'm absolutely sure."

"What do you want me to do about it?"

Vicki flushed. "I—I don't know, sir. But I don't like the way Neff is acting. Alert, sort of—guarded. It makes me uneasy."

The pilot reminded her that he had to be very sure something was amiss. He could not afford to take action, and possibly antagonize an innocent passenger.

"We still have time. Let's not go off half cocked. If anything develops, let me know."

"Yes, sir," Vicki said, despairing. She left and walked quickly past Mr. Neff.

She had just got back to her jump seat, and sat down for the first time since the flagship left New York, when the interphone sounded.

"Come up here, please," said Jackson's voice.

Vicki balanced her way up the swaying aisle. She had to pass Neff once more. The thin man *was* watching her. He made no effort, now, to conceal his interest in all these trips to the pilot.

Up in the half-dark pilot's cabin again, Vicki looked at the empty sky and whirling propellers. She wondered if she was not dreaming this whole adventure.

Jackson said, "Joe here has an idea. Tell her."

The young copilot said, "I agree with you, Vicki, that we oughtn't to take chances with men like these. At the very least, we ought to notify New York and ask them to check on who these men are. Or who this Neff is."

"I'm glad you agree with me," Vicki said. "But we're a long way out of New York—checking would take time, and maybe produce nothing. Shouldn't we notify Washington?"

The plane roared ahead while the pilot thought.

"We still have a few minutes to Washington," he said. "I'll decide and let you know. Don't worry, Vicki."

"Yes, Captain." Vicki went out.

She had no sooner stepped into the passenger cabin than Neff beckoned to her.

"Come here, Miss Barr."

"Yes, Mr. Neff?"

"The pilots certainly keep you girls busy," he said conversationally. "You've made a lot of trips up there in a short time."

"Oh, the pilots need the logbook, and express pouch and—and they're curious to know if the riding is smooth back here," she rushed on, flustered, "and what passengers they're carrying on this trip, and—"

She had said the wrong thing. Neff looked at her searchingly.

"So they're curious about the passengers, are they?"

"Sometimes we have celebrities aboard—" Vicki faltered.

The thin man looked at her with eyes of ice. His whole face hardened, but his voice remained smooth.

"Will you get me a glass of water, Miss Barr?"

"Certainly, sir."

She went back and entered the galley and poured a glass of water. Turning to carry it out, she found John Neff, still carrying his brief case, standing in the galley door. He blocked her way.

"I think you've made enough trips up to the pilot," he said dryly.

"I don't understand, Mr. Neff."

"You understand me perfectly," he snapped. "I'm not going to let you get to the pilot again! You've probably said something already. But you're not going to say any more. You're going to stay right here in the kitchen where you can't talk!"

He braced one arm across the narrow galley opening so that there was no possibility of Vicki's getting out. Up ahead, the passengers could hear nothing. If they did chance to turn around and look back, they would merely see the tall, thin man chatting with the stewardess in the galley. She was trapped.

The interphone buzzed. Vicki's hopes leaped. The phone was just outside the galley door, just beyond Neff's shoulder. Vicki started to reach out a hand. Neff laid a firm hand on her wrist.

"Let it ring," he said. "Don't try anything. Or you'll be very, very sorry."

The interphone continued to buzz. Vicki had to stand there and let it go unanswered. Then it stopped ringing. They flew on, to Washington. And at Washington, Vicki knew, Neff would disappear. She looked down helplessly at her wrist watch and saw the minutes tick past.

Suddenly the copilot was standing behind Neff.

"Why didn't you answer our buzz, Vicki? What's wrong?"

Then he looked at Neff, filling the doorway, at Vicki backed into the galley, and grasped the situation at once.

"So that's it." The copilot picked up the receiver of the interphone. Neff made a move to stop him but was not fast enough.

"Jackson," said the copilot, looking angrily at Neff. "You'd better get that message off. Take my word for it, it's urgent."

Neff's face flushed with rage. Vicki was alarmed. But the copilot did not care whether or not Neff knew that the pilot was radioing ahead for police to meet the plane.

"Go to your seat," he ordered Neff. "We're coming down now."

Neff turned and sullenly went up the aisle to his seat.

The copilot put his hand on Vicki's shoulder. "You all right? Had a nasty scare, didn't you? Don't worry, I'm looking out for you."

Vicki breathed her thanks. "But this isn't over yet!"

"I know. Keep a sharp watch when we land. Strap in now, Vicki."

Vicki strapped and the copilot hurried up forward to assist with the landing.

They circled over the white buildings. As Vicki sat tensely in her jump seat, she determined on one thing.

"Never mind the routine duties. The big thing is to keep Neff from disappearing!"

They were down. The passenger agent opened the door. Passengers streamed down the slanting aisle and clustered at the door. Vicki stood there at the door, waiting for Neff to come by. He seemed very tall, very thin, as he passed her, staring ahead.

Vicki followed his gaze. Neff was looking at two watchful men in dark suits, standing near the plane's portable steps.

Neff came down the stairs, keeping close behind a man and a woman. He ducked his head, as if trying to disguise his height. The two men below edged nearer.

Quietly, so quietly that no one but Vicki noticed, the two FBI men stepped up to Neff and took him in custody. He did not resist, but stood meekly between them. They motioned to Vicki. "Follow us."

Neff went along quietly between the two FBI men.

Vicki followed, a little behind. They wove their way among the planes parked on the night field.

Without warning Neff made a break at a tangent and dashed in Vicki's direction. The two FBI men turned and gave instant chase. Vicki ran too. Neff had passed her and was just ahead of her, running off at an angle. Because of that angle, Vicki was slightly nearer to Neff than the FBI men.

Fleetly she raced after the running shadow that was Neff. Her hair whipped out behind her as she loped across the aprons, and dodged baggage trucks.

Neff zigzagged. The FBI men and Vicki zigzagged, her quick eyes never losing him. He still held the brief case tightly under his arm. He fled around the tail of a parked plane. Vicki gained on him. At the wing of the parked plane, he looked back over his shoulder, running madly, blindly— Vicki shrieked. Her voice was drowned out.

The parked plane was warming up. Its propellers were revving! Straight toward the invisible propellers the thin man ran. If he ran into those whirling steel blades, he would be killed!

Vicki redoubled her speed. "Stop! The propellers!" she yelled, panting for breath. She was close enough now to Neff to see him gasping— One more spurt of speed—if she could summon up one more spurt— She could see the faint white blur of spinning propellers, and the tall thin gray figure silhouetted against them.

She reached out, grabbed the tail of his coat and caught him, and dragged him back.

"The propellers," she gasped, holding with all her strength onto his coat. "Move away—"

He was ashen as he looked and realized what he had just escaped. "But the—the—" He stared at the FBI men rushing toward him. "Let me go!"

He tried to wrench free of Vicki. She held on, clinging like a bulldog.

The two men bore down on them, and seized and handcuffed Neff.

"All right, miss. We've got him."

She nodded wearily. She was free. She started to walk back to her own plane, when one of the FBI men called out to her:

"You'll be wanted for questioning."

CHAPTER XIII

Street of Shadows

HOW PETE CARMODY GOT WIND OF THE BURTON-MORRIS-
Neff affair, Vicki never knew. But the young newspaperman was at the New York airport at noon to
meet her on her return—comically battered hat, grin,
and all.

"Vicki, you're terrific!" He had got on board the
emptied plane with her while she made her final
check. "Here, honey, somebody's left a pair of gloves.
Now tell me about it! Golly, that was swell, what you
did!"

Vicki put her tongue in her cheek. "As if you were
interested in what I did. You just want to scoop a story
for your paper."

He seized her hands and looked at her earnestly.
"You have no idea in that little head how interested I
am." Pete's eyes were very brown and honest. Vicki
lowered her own gaze.

"I'd be glad to give you the story, Pete—and I will give it to you first—but I was instructed not to talk just yet. The FBI hasn't closed the case. Besides, I don't know myself what it's all about." She grinned. "Believe me, I'm bursting to talk—about what little I saw with my own eyes."

"Sounds like some big racket, all right," Pete said. "Well, when the story does break, you're certainly going to be a heroine. I'll see to it personally that your picture gets on the front page. Don't laugh! And don't you ever dare think," he added fiercely, "that I'd put a story ahead of you. If I ever do such a thing, you can sue me!"

They both laughed.

"You can have your hands back now," said Pete, letting her go. He sighed. "There are times when I regret that I'm a gentleman."

"If you want to be a super-de luxe gentleman, you can take me home. Honestly, Pete, I'm topsy-turvy from everything that's happened. Praise be, I have several days off to rest."

Back at the apartment, Vicki had no chance to rest. The girls were all home together, except Dot, and they pestered Vicki to talk about that mysterious matter Ruth Benson was so excited about. Ruth Benson had mentioned the FBI—the girls knew that much. Vicki's protests of enforced silence, sleepiness, and just plain stubbornness did no good. Jean pulled her blonde hair.

Celia begged and pouted, even Charmion teased to be told. Tessa was sure Vicki would be a celebrity. Only Mrs. Duff said, "Let the lass alone. Shoo!"

Vicki did tell them this much: "I'll be called for further questioning by the FBI. Now will you please forget I exist?"

She took a nap that afternoon, as per regulations, and dreamed of four men wearing rubies, and of planes that dived in the night over Chickasaw Street. She must have cried out in her sleep, for Charmion shook her and said:

"Stop it, Vicki! Stop it! You're only dreaming."

Vicki rubbed her blue eyes. Then she sat up, clasping her knees. "This spooky affair must be preying on the Barr mind."

Charmion nodded. "More than you realize."

"As a tracker-downer of dubious characters, I guess I'm not so nonchalant, at that. Funny, Charmion. While it was all happening—forgive me for not telling you what 'it' was—I was scared a little, but only a little. Now that it's over, I'm scared pink and blue."

"Because having the FBI come to the scene made you realize what dangerous business you had strolled into."

"FBI! Who'd have thought it!" Vicki exclaimed. "Nice, quiet, routine runs and I end up in the arms of the law." She shook her radiant head. "Wonder what the FBI wants of me next. Wonder if I'll ever learn the whole story."

"I'm sure you will," Charmion said, and she sounded so comforting that Vicki kissed her.

Mrs. Duff poked her gray head in to say that there was a long-distance call for Miss Victoria Marvell Barr from Fairview.

"From home!"

Vicki jumped up delightedly and got to the telephone in record speed.

"Hello, you adventurer," said her mother's voice. "Ginny and I grew so lonesome for you that we thought we'd call you up."

"Though why we should miss *you* is an open question," said Ginny's acerbic voice. "I'm on the upstairs extension. Hi, Vicki. Remember me?"

"Hello, hello, both of you darlings!" Vicki said joyously. "How are you, anyway?"

"Blooming."

"Flourishing. Are *you* all right?"

"Are you having adventures?"

Vicki laughed. "I'm having such adventures that your hair will stand on end when you read about them in the newspapers! . . . Yes, me, your own sprout, in the newspapers. Of course I'm all right, Mother . . . Yes, I *am* . . . No, I'm sorry, I can't tell you yet what happened . . . In a few days . . . Better prepare Dad for the lurid details or he'll make me come home and devote my life to embroidering doilies. How's Dad?"

"Fine," said Betty Barr. "Working hard at the university. Cooking like mad, as usual. He said to give you his love."

"He fixed shrimps Palooka or something, and I got sick," piped Ginny. "Are you going to be famous? Freckles is sleeping on your bed. He has fleas again. I hate school. Wish that torture chamber would burn down! Oh, yes, and I bought a pair of high-heeled shoes, like yours. The foot doctor said I could never be a ballet dancer unless my ankles grow stronger, so mother gave in and said I could wear the high heels around the house *only*—I teeter a good deal—and I'm going to be a dietitian instead. See?"

"I think I see," said Vicki. "So that flea trap Freckles is still sleeping on my nice little bed! . . . What? . . . Of course he may. I love him too."

"Vicki," said her mother, in that well-known tone of command.

"Yes, ma'am?"

"Dad and I want you to come home for a visit at your earliest opportunity. You've been away four months now, and we feel we must see you soon."

Ginny said blithely, "I'll come to New York and make a report on Vic. Aren't you in love *yet?*"

"Uh-uh. At least I don't think so. But I have two sweetie-pies hovering around . . . Dean and Pete

. . . Well, they don't look like Adonises, but you wouldn't hide them . . . No, I can't choose between them, Ginny. Do I *have* to choose? . . . All right, Mother, I'll try to get enough time off to fly home. Yes, soon, dear . . . Look for me in the newspapers!"

"In the comics," Ginny said. They exchanged fond good-byes and Vicki hung up.

She continued to sit there for a while beside the telephone, thinking of her family. What a gay and dear family they were! Even Freckles, fleas and all. She had wanted to tell her mother and little sister about this gooseflesh-raising affair. She hoped her father would not say, "Thumbs down on stewardess work for you!" when the FBI released the whole story.

"I'd like to read that story myself," she confided to Jean, as Mrs. Duff sent them scampering to wash their hands and powder their noses for dinner.

"It won't be long now," Jean replied. "Tell the FBI I noticed one of those brief cases on my plane, too. What do you suppose was in it? Might tell the FBI that Cox always did have a yen to be a detective."

The one person Vicki could talk most freely with, about this affair, and the only one who had not showed up yet, was Dean Fletcher. The copilot was out on a flight. He came to the apartment next day.

In the living room he hurried over to Vicki and anxiously scanned her from fair head to frivolously shod feet.

"Sir, I am all right," Vicki said. "Now please sit down."

Dean dropped into the big chair. It was none too big for this tall, lean boy. He leaned back and shut his serious eyes for an instant.

"I tell you, Vicki," he said, "when the grapevine brought me this gossip I was worried."

They exchanged weak grins.

"Were you really worried about me?" Vicki teased. "Honestly?"

"Yes. I felt bad. I thought, 'If little Vicki should—' Never mind." He looked embarrassed. "We'll skip that one too."

Then, in a more serious tone, Dean said, "I have a message for you via the airport. Sort of confidential. You're to go to the FBI offices at Foley Square this afternoon at four. At seven tonight, be on the Memphis plane."

"Whee! Four, then seven. Working my way down, or riding like a lady?"

"You'll go as a passenger. Tom Jordan and I are the crew. Jean Cox is stewardess. She's probably just hearing about it now." He rose. "See you at seven."

She accompanied him to the door. "I'm glad it'll be you three. I'm especially glad it'll be you."

"Are you?" To her surprise, Dean bent down and kissed her, gravely, sweetly. "Till seven, Vic."

"Till seven, Dean."

After he closed the door, Vicki leaned against it, too amazed to move. Dean Fletcher—sisterless, girl-shy, unaware of anything more feminine than an engine— had kissed her!

"It was nice." She smiled happily at herself in the mirror, getting into her hat and coat. "I'm sure the FBI will be interested to hear all about it!"

In big, grim, gray offices, the FBI asked Vicki to go through a file of photographs and pick out, if she could, the first three men.

It took a long time. It was hard to decide about Burton One, or even Burton Two, among so many photographs. She identified Charles Morris's photograph without much hesitation.

"That will be all, Miss Barr. Thank you."

"But in Memphis tonight—?" she asked.

"You will be met in Memphis."

It was fun flying at leisure, with time to look down on the evening landscape and the lighted cities below. Vicki pretended to gloat over Jean, and demanded all sorts of impossible services, such as a shower, an ice-cream soda, and an introduction to busy copilot Fletcher. Vicki felt quite out of character when Jean put a tempting tray in her lap and tucked a blanket over her knees, against the cold. But she found herself craning her neck at stops, to see what Jean and the passenger agent were doing, and she missed being able to chat with all the pleasant-looking people riding this plane.

The evening wore on. Vicki chatted with Jean, whenever Jean was free. The rest of the time she studied an air map and tried to figure varying winds and speeds from the way they were flying tonight. These was no moon; it was too dark to see much outside her little plane window. On the last lap of the journey, between midnight and 2:30, Vicki tried to sleep. She might run into all sorts of surprises at Memphis and she wanted to be wide awake, with her wits about her. But though she pushed back her upholstered chair to reclining position, sleep would not come. Vicki was too excited about whatever she was to encounter, in a matter of minutes now.

Jean came by. "Memphis in five minutes, Vic."

"I hope you and Dean can come with me."

"Doubt it. You'll probably have to go alone. Oh! Dean sends you a message. He says, take care of yourself and watch out for newspapermen."

"He does, does he?" Vicki's eyes sparkled for a moment. Then she put on her hat and coat and gloves, sat down again, and strapped in for the landing.

It was strange to get off at the Memphis airfield without being a member of the crew, without knowing where she was going. Vicki had never been here on her own before; she felt a little forlorn. Sleepy passengers straggled off the plane, new ones got on, and Vicki stood waiting to be met. Dean, Jean, and Captain Jordan lingered at a tactful distance, not wanting to leave her all alone.

Two men, in inconspicuous dark suits, came up. They showed their badges. Vicki could not see their faces well under their hats, in this black night, but their voices were friendly.

"You are Victoria Barr? Come with us, please." They did not give her their names. Vicki turned and waved to her three friends, then hastened off with the G-men.

They stepped into a car in which a driver was waiting. Vicki sat between the two men and they questioned her briefly. They were big, easy-mannered, capable men, and Vicki felt that, whatever happened, she was safe with them.

But her hopes of adventure were immediately dashed, for the G-men said:

"We are going to want you to identify some people. We won't take you along now, because it might be dangerous. But you stay on tap, at the hotel."

They escorted Vicki into her usual hotel and drove away. Vicki was left behind, fuming, in a dull hotel room.

"I can guess where they're going!" she thought. "It must be to Chickasaw Street!"

She plumped down on the bed, rebellious at being left behind.

"Gosh, if I have to stay here and wait I'll burst with curiosity!"

She went downstairs to the deserted lobby and left word with the desk clerk that she was going out for a sandwich. Out on the dark street, she found a cab at the curb and got in.

"Chickasaw Street," she said.

About a block from the jewelry store they had noticed that night, Vicki directed the driver to stop. She paid him, got out, and walked the final block. The street was still, drab, and as grim as she had remembered it, a street of shadows. This street was high on the Chickasaw bluffs and below she could see the Mississippi. The stillness made the back of her neck prickle. Instinctively she walked close to the buildings, keeping in shadow.

An arm reached out. It was one of the G-men who had met her at the airport.

"What are you doing here?" he said in annoyance.

Vicki explained, his stern tone making her feel apologetic.

The second FBI man shook his head, but said, "As long as you're here, all right. There's no one to take you back now. You've just walked into what's going to be a surprise raid, young lady. Keep behind us, and identify the men when we ask you."

The G-men, Vicki behind them, passed the garishly lighted and noisy coffee shop. They passed the jewelry shop, with the same dim light in its window, and the same tawdry wares. Vicki did not know what to expect next.

"Keep behind us," came the whispered order.

The two G-men turned into the alley beside the jewelry shop, walking soundlessly in the dust. Vicki followed. She stole a look over her shoulder. Her eyes, accustomed now to the dense shadows, picked out men lurking in the darkest spots, up and down the block. Three . . . four . . . five men—perhaps there were more, even right here in the alley. They were all facing the obscure jewelry shop. Covering it, she realized, and armed.

So softly and quickly that Vicki did not expect it, the G-men unlocked the door leading from the alley and opened it. Instantly they leveled guns.

Light spilled out through the open doorway, illuminating the dusty alley and the guns in the G-men's hands. Two more men had noiselessly come up behind them, to join them. Beyond, where the light was, in a sort of small stockroom, Morris, and the two Burtons sat around a table. Their faces showed complete surprise. Slowly their hands went up over their heads, without a word spoken. With them sat an elderly little man, looking badly frightened. On the table lay the ostrich-hide brief cases, opened, many small chamois bags, large cardboard and metal boxes, an inventory sheet, magnifying glasses, and cutting tools. Vicki saw all this in a flash, but still did not understand.

The two G-men entered, Vicki behind them. The powdery, Oriental fragrance Vicki had smelled near those brief cases now was overpowering in the room.

"Are these the men you spotted in transit, Miss Barr?"

"Yes . . . yes, they are, sir."

"Name them."

Vicki looked into their hate-filled faces and hesitated. The gun in the G-man's hand moved forward a few inches, and held steady, right beside her.

Vicki pointed. "Morris. Burton, and—ah—Burton. I never saw the old man before."

"They all carried these brief cases on your plane?"

"Yes, sir."

"Good, that's what we want to know. That clinches our case."

One of the men behind Vicki gave a low whistle through the open alleyway door. Footsteps sounded out on the sidewalk, as the men in ambush emerged from the shadow, and an automobile engine purred.

Suddenly Morris got to his feet and knocked over the table. The lights went out. Something heavy—a chair or a stool—came hurtling toward Vicki and crashed on the wall.

G-men instantly trained flashlights on the four. Guns spat flame and roared. The fight was so fast, at such close range, that to Vicki it was only deadly confusion. A man seized her from behind and yanked her out into the alley. She crouched there, hearing the yells, the crashing furniture, men fighting in the dark. Guns blazed again.

Windows in Chickasaw Street were thrown up, and neighbors started to scream. A police siren wailed distantly, racing nearer. Then lights went on again in the jewelry shop. There was a sickening silence, groans, then low words of command.

Trembling, Vicki moved toward the lighted doorway to look. She saw Morris, bloody, his suit half torn off. One of the G-men who had met her was painfully clasping his side. The others were disheveled, panting, but furiously calm, holding the four men captive at gunpoint. The back room of the shop was a shambles.

And scattered thickly over the floor, like the legendary paving stones of heaven, lay great shimmering diamonds, rubies, deep blue sapphires, winking yellow topazes, green uncut jade, and pearls like snow of the Orient.

CHAPTER XIV

Smugglers

THE REST WENT SWIFTLY.

Vicki was driven to FBI headquarters, away from Chickasaw Street. The last she saw of the four men, they were handcuffed and being taken away in cars. She knew she would never see Morris and the two Burtons again.

The night was beginning to fade as Vicki and the two FBI men who had met her climbed stone steps into a stone building. A guard unlocked the barred door for them. They walked along echoing corridors, and Vicki peered in at offices that never slept: telephone and international cable switchboards, men bent over desks.

"In here, Miss Barr."

She was shown into a private office, where a portly man, obviously in charge, sat talking into a telephone.

The phone, she noticed as the man hung up, was rigged with a silencer to keep his calls secret. He rose and enveloped Vicki's hand in a huge handshake.

"I'm Inspector Reynolds. Sit down. You've been a great help to us, Miss Barr. Very brave, even though you spoiled our attempt to keep you out of danger. Sit down, Mac. Dave, you go get that wound dressed right away." The wounded man left.

Vicki sank wearily into an office chair. "I'm glad if I was of help, Mr. Reynolds—though I don't understand how."

He smiled a little. "I'll explain. You have every right to an explanation." He buzzed for a male secretary and asked for hot coffee for all of them. Then Mr. Reynolds hitched his chair away from his desk, closer to Vicki and Mac, and said:

"The story started in San Francisco, with an importer named Carter. Carter operated a legitimate business importing jute cloth and hemp, coarse silk, rugs, and hides from India."

"Including ostrich hides?" Vicki asked.

"Yes. I'll come to those brief cases in a minute."

"This business was a 'front,' an innocent façade to conceal what was going on. In Carter's bales and crates were secreted uncut rubies, uncut jade, some cut diamonds, some pearls. These jewels were smuggled in without paying tariff to the United States government. Saving the cost of customs duties, the jewels could then be sold within the United States at enormous profit.

"But evading the revenue laws is a very serious offense," the inspector went on. "The smugglers had to work with caution in disposing of their illegally obtained jewels. They went to great pains.

"Carter, the importer, distributed the jewels in small quantities among several men who traveled. Three such agents were Morris and the two men called Burton; there were others. These agents brought the jewels to a man in New York who was the real head of the smuggling ring. That man was John Neff."

Vicki gasped. "Neff was the headman!"

"Yes. He operated secretly in a 'blind' office in New York. He directed and co-ordinated the work of the agents, who carried jewels all over the country. Neff's directives were never written or telegraphed. They were given always in person or by long-distance telephone, so that he left no traces.

"Neff received, appraised, and inventoried all the uncut gems coming in from the West Coast importer. In fact, Neff is considered a jewel expert. He is also a good deal of a fop. He sported quite a ruby, himself. Those fancy ostrich-hide brief cases were a conceit of his. He took the raw skins sent from India and had them manufactured into brief cases here. You know those brief cases were stuffed with jewels, don't you?"

Vicki's blue eyes widened.

"Yes, each brief case contained thousands of dollars' worth of gems."

The FBI chief went on to describe Neff's system. "After appraising and listing the raw gems, Neff redistributed them, in small quantities, among the agents, with instructions. Neff kept track of the whereabouts of the traveling agents and gems. He co-ordinated the agents' movements: they could locate one another and meet if necessary by telephoning Neff in New York. Neff also performed one more function: he prepared fake documents about the origins of these jewels, 'showing' that a jewel came from an estate, to satisfy buyers that these were legitimate, not stolen, goods."

"But where did the agents go?" Vicki asked. "How could they sell an uncut ruby, for example? Uncut stones aren't often offered for sale, are they? People would be suspicious, I should think."

"Right. The agents occasionally sold the gems in their uncut state, but it was too risky. Generally, what they did was to take the stones to small, obscure, trusted jewelers in various towns, and have the gems cut and set. In that way," Mr. Reynolds said, "the agents could then sell 'blind' articles, innocent-seeming pieces of jewelry."

Mac put in: "You see, Miss Barr, you wouldn't think of buying a handful of loose, unmatched, unpolished pearls, even at a bargain, without asking a lot of questions. Neither would a jeweler, if he was honest or in his right mind. But if someone offered to sell you a pearl necklace, and produced a document showing it came from, say, a shop that had gone out of business— why, it'd never occur to you that you were receiving stolen or smuggled goods. For which, of course, you're liable for a jail sentence."

"I see," said Vicki. "So Neff and the agents had the smuggled gems cut and set, by various jewelers."

"The ring's jewelers who did the cutting," Mr. Reynolds continued, "were several, and were in scattered parts of the United States. This was because the ring considered it too risky to keep all the smuggled jewels in any one city, or in any one person's hands. The jewels were kept scattered, so that if one cutter or one agent was caught, not all the gems would be seized, but only a few.

"Also, the jewels were kept scattered and in circulation throughout the country because this facilitated sales. Sales had to be quick—and in small quantities, only one or two pieces at a time, to avert suspicion— and preferably to small, individual, honest jewelers in smaller towns. The latter would not be so well informed as to sources of gems and thus not so suspicious as the big jewelry houses in New York.

"The part of the game which you saw, Miss Barr," the portly man said, "was the agents flying uncut gems from New York to Memphis to be cut. From Memphis, they carried out the finished pieces of jewelry, and traveled along the Mississippi into smaller towns to sell them."

Mac spoke up. "The old man you saw tonight in the shop was one of their cutters."

"We've had our eye on these smugglers and their illegal traffic for a long time," the inspector continued, "but we needed to prove they and the jewels were in transit. That's where your testimony came in. You have clinched the case."

"Mr. Reynolds," Vicki said, "I'm wondering about that time at the Washington stop—when the two Burtons changed places. They met in the washroom and switched clothes, didn't they?"

"That's right," Mac said. "That brief case was literally worth its weight in diamonds. You understand those stones were 'hot' goods—could be seized by the police if spotted—and had to be delivered to the Memphis cutter and secreted and converted in a hurry."

Mr. Reynolds explained that, through Neff's coordination, agents coming from different directions often met en route to pass on jewels and information.

Vicki's soft blue eyes were speculative. "Now I understand why those men never opened their brief cases and never wanted to talk to me—except Neff, when he was cornered." She remembered Charles Morris and the Seeing Eye dog who had sniffed the powdery fragrance.

"Mr. Reynolds, what was that Oriental scent, anyway? I always smelled it near those ostrich-hide brief cases. And again in the jewelry shop tonight—it was so strong there—"

"The uncut gems were kept in cotton and in a special Oriental talcum. They arrived from India wrapped that way, to protect them. That talcum is what you smelled. The brief cases were lined with silk and chamois. That's what made them a trifle bulky. And the locks—you probably noticed those complicated locks on the cases."

"And my fourth passenger," Vicki went on remembering. "Neff himself!"

"Neff did not usually travel," Mr. Reynolds said. "But he wanted to check inventories with the Memphis cutter. He didn't trust this particular cutter. As long as Neff was coming down here to Memphis, he carried along a packet of gems. Incidentally, they always flew on the night run, you noticed. Their whole business was conducted in the middle of the night to ensure the greatest secrecy. The agents didn't want to be seen going into these out-of-the-way jewelry shops."

Vicki recalled the time she and Dean had trailed Burton to Chickasaw Street, but lost him.

"He disappeared because he ducked into the alley. He had a key to that alley door which leads into the back of the shop. He let himself in, and that's why you lost him."

Mac said, "That alley entrance to the jewelry shop made our surprise raid a lot easier. We took wax impressions of the lock in that door, and had a skeleton key made. Then, as you saw, we got in easily tonight."

"The two Burtons and Morris met tonight because they hadn't heard from Neff—since we caught him at the Washington airport."

Vicki's eyes were heavy. She grinned and admitted, "I can't think of any more questions to ask."

"That's because you know the full story now," Mr. Reynolds said kindly.

Mac brought her her coat. Both men thanked Vicki warmly for her help, and congratulated her on the courage she had shown.

A staff car and chauffeur drove her to the hotel where the crew was staying. Vicki rode along in the pale, early daylight, seeming to see again the blazing profusion of jewels on the floor. The night's happenings were fantastic, and yet it had all happened. To her!

"This is what I get for being a flight stewardess," was her last amazed thought as she climbed into bed when the rest of the city was getting up for breakfast.

CHAPTER XV

Home in Triumph

NOW VICKI WAS A HEROINE IN EARNEST. THE STORY BROKE
and a huge picture of Vicki, in her airline uniform, was
plastered over the front of the Memphis newspaper.
For that matter, Vicki smiled out from the front pages
of papers all over the country. FLIGHT STEWARDESS
CATCHES JEWEL SMUGGLERS! the headlines shrieked.
BLONDE AIR HOSTESS CORNERS CRIMINAL IN AIR!

Vicki sat alone in her Memphis hotel room, sur-
rounded by a sea of newspapers, and absolutely appalled. Captain Jordan had ordered the newspapers
sent up to her, along with lunch "—in case you don't
feel like facing the public just yet, Vicki."

She certainly did not feel like going down into the
lobby, where she would be stared at. Captain Jordan,
Dean, and Jean Cox had had to work their flight back
to New York, and had gone without her. Vicki rather
dreaded returning to New York, facing the other stew-

ardesses' questions, the inevitable publicity, the airline officials' questions. She was tired after this great adventure. Her eye fell again on the screaming headlines.

"What's being blonde got to do with it?" Vicki fumed to herself. "I hate all this fuss! Gosh, it's still only *me*."

At that moment the telephone in her room rang.

Vicki shut her eyes in chagrin and braced herself for official questions. But it turned out to be Ruth Benson, who blessedly said:

"Vicki, I've just heard the whole story this morning. Congratulations! We're all very proud of you! But I know you must need a rest. I've arranged a breathing spell for you. Don't come back to New York. Go right home to Fairview from Memphis. Federal will give you a free flight, of course."

"Thank you, thank you!"

Miss Benson chuckled. "I thought you'd like to be home after all this excitement."

Vicki was greatly relieved. The more she thought about the immediate prospect of seeing The Castle and her family the more delighted and excited she became. She wasted no time in phoning the Memphis airport and asking if they could find space for her on the very next Federal plane. They could. She wired her family. Vicki wasted no time on packing either—she had only her toothbrush and nightgown to pack. Most of her clothes, the nice things she would have liked to wear at home were hanging in the closet of the New York apartment. Well, she would just have to arrive home in her flight uniform.

"Perhaps that won't be so bad," Vicki thought, as she dashed out into the hotel corridor and kept her finger on the elevator buzzer. "The family's never seen me in uniform—they'll be interested, even if amazed."

From Memphis Vicki flew to Cleveland, and at the Cleveland airport changed to another plane for the long flight to Chicago. It was evening when she arrived. She wired her family that she would be home in short order, then hopped the local train down to Fairview. Knowing that Professor Barr had probably cooked the fatted calf in her honor, Vicki was careful not to eat so much as a peanut.

As the train slid into Fairview's little railroad station, Vicki glimpsed through the train window her family standing on the platform. Professor and Mrs. Barr were both bundled into their topcoats, eagerly scanning the cars. Ginny wore a great red hairbow for the occasion. Freckles sported a red bow on his collar but was trying to chew it off.

Vicki jumped off the train and ran straight into three pairs of waiting arms.

"Oh, I'm so glad to see you all!" she exclaimed. "So happy!"

"How are you, Victoria?"

"How are *you?*"

"Look at Vicki in her flight uniform!" Ginny shrieked. "It's stunning! Makes her look like someone I wish I knew! Can I try it on?"

"Well, not here on the platform, baby."

"I've cooked a magnificent dinner for you, Vicki!"

"Come, get into the car." Betty Barr laughed. "Someone catch Freckles—he's so excited, he's running in circles."

Home at The Castle, they feasted and talked and laughed until late into the night. Her family could hardly believe what an adventure Vicki had just been through. Vicki was concerned because it worried her parents, and had to reassure them over and over again —particularly Professor Barr—that stewardess work ordinarily was not risky. "And it's at least as educational as college!" Vicki asserted.

Mrs. Barr shook her short curls. "I expect you're learning a great deal," she agreed. "Vicki, I almost envy you. If I were twenty years younger, I'd apply for stewardess work myself!"

"I wouldn't let you go." Professor Barr smiled. "I've lost one of my girls—isn't that enough?"

"You can't lose me, Dad," Vicki said, getting up and going around the table to hug him. "What are you going to cook for me tomorrow?"

Betty Barr said firmly, "*I* am going to cook tomorrow, and all this week. Dad had his field day tonight. Besides, Vicki, I suspect tomorrow you'll be too busy to think of menus."

"What's up?"

"Tell you tomorrow, dear. Now, don't you think it's time you and Ginny went to bed?"

"Good heavens," said Professor Barr, "has anyone noticed that it is now one-thirty in the morning?"

"That's because we've been having fun," Vicki said happily. "Good night, parents," she added, kissing them. "C'mon, Ginny."

The two girls trudged upstairs, Ginny lugging the spaniel. In their blue room, it took them a very long time to get to bed. First, Vicki had to inspect the hooked rug Ginny had made, and the place where Freckles had scratched the woodwork. Then they had to hang out the window and have a look at the garden, and the lake beyond. Then Ginny had to try on Vicki's flight uniform. It was too large for her in some places, and too tight in others, so Vicki obligingly pinned here and draped there. Thus Ginny was able to admire herself in the dressing-table mirror and declare:

"Just wait a few years! Then I'm going to give you some real competition."

They climbed into their twin beds at last. But Vicki crawled out again, remembering a sheet and envelope of airline stationery she had picked up for Ginny on the Chicago plane. Then Ginny remembered that she wanted to show Vicki her new high-heeled shoes, her first, a far too important matter to wait until morning. Then, with lights out again, Freckles decided to play tag by himself across both their beds and stomachs. It was three o'clock by the time they all finally settled down.

Vicki slept late. She awoke to find her blue room flooded with sunshine, Ginny's bed empty, and her mother peeking in at the door.

"He's here!"

"Who's here?" Vicki demanded.

"Didn't I tell you last night? Mr. Peter Carmody. He flew out to get an exclusive interview with you for his newspaper."

Vicki leaned back against the pillows and howled with laughter. The spectacle of herself and Pete acting as dignified public characters, interviewing and being interviewed, was too much.

"Tell him I'll be right down," she gasped.

"You will be down in due time," said her father, edging into the room. He bore an enormous breakfast tray and set it on Vicki's knees.

"Lewis!" exclaimed his wife, laughing. "There's everything on that tray but the crown jewels!"

On the tray was a profusion of individual casseroles, Mrs. Barr's best silver coffeepot and linen, the luster "thousand faces" dishes from China and—compliments of Ginny—a geranium.

"It's beautiful, Dad," Vicki said gratefully. "Thank you ever so much!" She peeped into the casseroles. "Looks marvelous! I suggest we *all* have lunch on what's on this tray. Including Pete—where is he?"

"Ginny is entertaining him," her mother said.

"She has him back in the garage fixing her bicycle, I believe," Professor Barr said. "Try the kidney stew, Victoria. Pete and Ginny were talking about giving a performance with the Walkers' pony next."

Knowing that Pete's high jinks could match even Ginny's, Vicki peacefully went to work on the tray. Some of her father's concoctions were on the exotic side, particularly for an empty stomach. But knowing that he would feel hurt if she did not appreciate his efforts, Vicki ate until she was ready to burst. Then she bathed and dressed and went downstairs in search of Pete Carmody and her little sister.

The telephone interrupted her. It was her roommates, extravagantly calling long-distance with their congratulations and questions.

"Miss Barr, we think you're pretty special," came Jean Cox's merry voice. "So do your passengers. Why, flowers and candy and gifts are simply pouring into the apartment and into Miss Benson's office for you—even from passengers who rode with you months ago!"

Vicki gulped and asked Jean to eat the candy for her.

"Vicki!" Charmion came on the wire next. "Vicki dear, I'm so proud of you! And do you know what? Ruth Benson is giving you a new assignment. . . . No, I'm sorry, I don't know what it is, but Benny says it's grand. . . . Well, yes," Charmion admitted modestly, "I'm getting a new assignment, too. Here's Tessa, hold on—"

Tessa was almost shrieking with excitement. "Vicki!

Vicki Barr! Why aren't you here in New York? How can you walk out on your big scene? You don't really want to turn your back on the spotlight?"

There was a pause and jumbled voices came out of the receiver. Mrs. Duff's crisp voice came through.

"Lass, I'm glad ye're home. It's bedlam here. Get a good rest now, mind!"

"Thanks, Mrs. Duff, I will."

Dot Crowley boomed over the wire. "Vicki, I do congratulate you. With a feat like this to increase your prestige, why, you can push your career ahead by leaps and bounds!"

By this time Vicki's head was in such a whirl that she began to laugh. "Thank you, thank you, all of you! Eat the candy and wear the flowers and tell Miss Benson that I can hardly wait to find out what she has in store for me!"

"So long, sweetie," Jean called. "See you soon!"

Vicki sat for a moment beside the telephone, at the foot of the tower stairs, thinking affectionately of her friends. Then she remembered that Pete and Ginny were waiting for her.

They were talking sedately with Mrs. Barr in the long living room. Pete stood up politely when Vicki entered, but he could not help clowning just the same.

"Vicki, what a place this Castle is! Marry me and we'll live here. No, no, really, Mrs. Barr, I'm just joking!"

Betty Barr grinned. "We might take you in on approval, Peter, providing you promise not to cook. One fancy chef is enough."

The chef-professor himself entered and looked benignly at Pete. "This young man is his paper's expert on economics and industrial relations. Bet you didn't know that, Vicki."

Pete looked embarrassed but pleased. "Only the second expert, sir, and I generally write up rather dry stories. But since I know Vicki personally, my paper agreed to send me out here to interview her. You know, Vicki, you promised me a story!"

"I did indeed."

Vicki told her story, guided by Pete's questions, in fuller detail than she had related it to her family last night. Her parents listened to every word, and Ginny listened popeyed.

"Did he actually trap you in the galley?" Ginny demanded. "He threatened you— Vic, did he pull a gun?"

Vicki giggled. "No gun. What do you think this was, baby, the movies? But it was bad enough."

The young newspaperman was impressed too. He wrote down Vicki's account and when she had finished, he said gravely:

"You were a brave girl, Vicki. And you used your head. There's no question but what you made a valuable contribution toward solving that case."

"I wish," Mrs. Barr remarked, "that you had stayed in the hotel as the FBI instructed you, and not wandered out to Chickasaw Street."

"But then she never would have been in on the surprise raid!" Ginny said excitedly. "Gosh, Vicki, I'll bet the FBI loves you!"

"Well, I love you for giving me this marvelous story," Pete said. "Now tell me, what are you going to do next? New assignment? New adventures?"

Vicki smiled tantalizingly. "Ruth Benson hinted there's something new in store for me. As soon as I get back, in a few days. Wait and see!"

Professor Barr announced, "For the time being Vicki stays right here at The Castle and rests!"

But that would be for only a few days, Vicki knew, and already she was wondering about the next flights, the next experiences, to come.

Pete was flying back on the early evening plane. When he said good-bye to Vicki, he wore such a long face that she had to laugh.

"This isn't good-bye, Pete. This is only au 'voir—because I have lots of unfinished business. Give my love to Dean and the girls and tell them I'll be back—soon!"

VICKI BARR flies South to new adventure in the next volume, VICKI FINDS THE ANSWER. Don't miss this thrilling mystery-adventure story of how Vicki helps a runaway girl and lands in the middle of an unscrupulous plot.